ISABELLA

Kevin A. Woodward

For Charley, Joseph and Daisy

Because of Boo and Obi

?

1993

She climbed the stairs slowly as the tears streamed down her face. Her sobs echoed quietly, returning to her ears from the concrete walls and steps. Flight after flight she continued to climb, her trainers scuffing the edge of the occasional stair, causing her to stumble and take hold of the metal railing. It was cold in the stairwell and there were goosebumps on her bare arms, but they were not from the cold. She was terrified as she climbed, the thirteen years of her young life had been difficult enough without the ordeal of the last few months, and then finally tonight. As she made her way up the twenty stories she could hear the noises of the families living in the walls on the other side, the lives they were living, each with their own personal struggles. A raised voice, a laugh, a TV blaring out of one, a party of a dozen different voices in another. Her struggle was real, and today she had been tested beyond her ability to cope.

As she reached the landing on the 20th floor she walked through a door that had a broken padlock hanging from it. The door was beaten up, splintered at the bottom and graffiti sprayed all over it with the tags of the local gangs. The metal stairs that stood before her led to the roof. For years the padlock had been broken, the council neglecting to replace it as it inevitably would just be broken again. Despite the 20 flight climb she didn't pause, continuing up the stairs, her deep breaths echoing even louder in the narrow stairwell. through the wooden door at the top and onto the roof.

The rain caught her hair, sticking it to her face, soaking her t-shirt as she walked along the fibre glass roof of the tower block. The cold November wind failed to phase her as it whipped around the rooftop outhouse she emerged from. Her tears washed away by the rain but her eyes burned red as she walked in a straight line towards the metal railing around the edge of the roof. It was at waist height and rusted, as she took it in both hands a shard of flaked paint cut her hand but she felt nothing, standing on the bottom rung she stepped over. There was another meter to the edge of the roof, without slowing she took two steps towards it, shivering and crying, and then she took a third ... and a fourth.

Monday, April 10th, 2016

It was on the morning of April 10th, 2016 that the video first appeared on YouTube. A new Youtuber, with no previous videos, and yet this video generated millions of views in the first couple of hours. It hit headlines, the morning news channels were dissecting it second by second, and soon after Scotland Yard was creating a task force to begin an investigation as crowds gathered near Trafalgar Square, unsure of the reality of the situation. Was it a fake? A weird publicity stunt? The chattering on buses and tubes during the morning commute called it everything from a prank to a movie trailer.

As the calls came into the 999 call centres from seven seemingly unrelated families, and the reality of the situation began to unfold, it started to dawn on the nation that the words in the video from the male voice were indeed sinister and real. The message that would shake the morality of every man and woman:

"My name is Malcolm. Over the next seven days, the people of Great Britain will search their souls for the answer to their innermost fears. Are you good people? Do you understand love and will you make the ultimate sacrifice for your nearest and dearest?

"I have placed a chair in the centre of Trafalgar Square. It's a simple wooden chair and until this moment served no real purpose, a chair that no one would have noticed before this week. But, in seven days, that chair will have played a part in the fate of seven people, for on that chair rests a gun, loaded with seven bullets. How many bullets left in the gun after seven days is up to the loved ones of these seven innocent people.

"During the night I have taken prisoner seven very carefully selected subjects. They have loved ones to whom I set this challenge. At 9pm each evening for the next seven days, you will take it in turns to walk up to the chair, pick up the gun and sit down. Place the barrel in your mouth and pull the trigger. Do this, and your loved one lives. Decline the invitation and your loved one dies. It's a simple game.

"The residents of Great Britain that I set this challenge to are as follows:

George Russ of 14 Hempstead Road, Whatford

Nicola Johnston of 247 Stag Lane, Edgware

Havinder (Harry) Singh of 28a Leicester Road, East Finchley

Claire Papadopolous of 112 Hewett Lane, Harringay

Martin Imbeault of 3 Gainsford Road, Walthamstow

Roy Ritchie of 81 Scholars Road, Chingford

And Michael Wenham of 44 Peartree Road, Enfield

"Please play the game in the order I have read out your names. For the sake of your loved ones I hope you make the right decision."

Sunday, April 9th, 2016

As George returned home from work, closing the front door with his elbow and dropping his keys on the side table in the corner, he frowned when his wife Wendy didn't reply to his usual jovial announcement. He walked past the living room throwing it a quick glance and headed into the kitchen where he normally found her perched on her stool watching the TV and simultaneously reading a magazine.

The magazine was open on an article about the bravery of an abused woman stabbing her husband, and the TV firmly tuned into the shopping channel. On the stove sat peeled potatoes in a pot, covered in water, and carrots in another but no gas-fired up beneath them. "Great," he thought "another late dinner." Returning to the hallway he called up the stairs and paused for a second, waited but there was no answer and so with a disgruntled mumble ascended expecting to find her dozing on the bed. Finding the rooms empty surprised him, and he fumbled for his phone in his pocket.

Dialing her number, he returned downstairs and walked into the living room, feeling perplexed as it went straight to her voicemail. "That's me home, not sure where you are … give me a call." He went back to the kitchen, glanced out the window at the back garden, and frowned when it was empty. He turned the gas on under both pots, opened the oven door to discover a pie, and turned the gas on that too. He paused for a second, checked his phone to see no calls, and went to sit in his armchair in the living room. Switching on the TV he tuned into Gold to watch the oldies, but his mind was distracted as Only Fools returned from an advert.

Their lives weren't 100% routine, but after sixteen years of marriage he generally knew she would be at home on a Sunday night, and he was sure she hadn't mentioned going anywhere. He pondered the un-boiled vegetables and cold oven, "why prepare it if she was going out?" It worked away at his conscious mind like an itch that slowly forms on the sole of your foot.

He considered the argument the night before, but they'd had worse in his opinion. She wouldn't have left because of that. He checked his phone again, nothing, opened his messages and sent her a text:

If you don't want to talk that's fine, I've put the veg on so it might be cold when you get in.

And placed the phone back on the arm of the chair. He almost expected an immediate buzz of the phone, but it just sat there refusing to vibrate. He continued to think about it on and off as Rodney and Delboy continued their antics, and eventually got up to stir the veg and potatoes. Fetching the drainer, he poured away the water, grabbed a plate and served himself, cutting a large slice of pie after carefully removing it from the oven.

Returning to the armchair, he even managed to laugh a little at the sketch on TV as he glanced up at the clock, flicking the TV over to the City game. Placing the plate on the coffee table he relaxed. "Fuck her, she'll come back when she's done sulking," he said out loud. But as the final whistle blew on a loss for his boys, he picked up his phone again. Nothing, no reply.

He phoned his sister in law, meddling bitch that she was, if Wendy was anywhere she was there.

"It's George, is my Wendy there?" he asked with as much of a smile as he could muster.

"Not seen her today George, she phoned me about lunchtime," the response was curt, there was mutual contempt between them that was barely veiled.

"Hmm, she was making dinner, must have popped out and hasn't returned," he didn't even doubt that the sister was telling the truth, following previous arguments she had gloated that Wendy was there and she wasn't coming back. "If you hear from her tell her to call me."

"She's probably seen the light George, time to learn how to use the washing machine," the chuckle was weak but sinister.

George managed a mumbled noise of contempt and hung up.

As 11pm approached he decided to phone 101. It's not an emergency, and he knew they would quote the expected "she's not a missing person until she's been gone 24 hours" but he spoke to them and left some details anyway. He then thumbed through to recently dialled numbers and called her again, voicemail immediately kicked in "Listen it's late, just come home, I love you, the door is unlocked just in case you don't have keys." He hung up and climbed the stairs to get ready for bed. "Maybe I went too far last night," he thought as he pulled over the duvet.

George woke with a bolt, turned over expecting Wendy to be lying there and stared at an empty pillow. "Bitch stayed out all night," his first impulsive response quickly turned to worry. She'd never been away all night unless she was at her sisters'. He swung his legs out of bed and ruffled his hair. A plan of action formed quickly which involved a shower and a lot of phone calls, and as he went towards the ensuite the inevitable buzz of his phone on the dresser made him smile.

"She'll have some groveling to do," he smirked as he pressed his thumb to unlock it. It wasn't from her, his mate Colin had tagged him in a video, he put the phone down, it was too early to watch dogs doing stupid things or workmen pranking each other. A shower is what he needed.

Freshened up, he got dressed, grabbed his phone and went to the kitchen to make a coffee. As the kettle boiled he glanced at his phone again, still nothing from Wendy. He shrugged it off, figuring she had checked into a hotel. He tapped on Colin's message:

You NEED to watch this now, I think this is you

There was a link to a YouTube video. He pressed play and turned up the audio.

Monday, April 10th, 8.15am

Two local beat cops were stood next to the wooden chair, ordering members of the public to get back as the armed police arrived. Within minutes a crime scene had been established with blue and white tape sectioning off a large part of Trafalgar Square. The crowd thickened on the other side of the tape, with photos being taken by the dozen and videos being streamed to all parts of the globe. Within two hours of the video being posted a couple of dozen police officers were at the scene, with plain-clothed detectives arriving alongside forensic examiners.

The calls into the emergency crisis centres had established that the names of the people mentioned in the video had mostly been in touch and scarily were all missing someone. This was not a hoax, this was very real. Amongst the crowd had arrived the media, vans and journalists and cameramen were setting up camp, a news story had revealed itself which could lead to being the most unique they had encountered.

A cop with body armour was inspecting the revolver, he identified it as a fully functional 386 revolver loaded with 7 live rounds. He spoke briefly with a detective.

"Leave it on the chair," the detective said, "there are clearly people missing, a wooden chair and a gun are at Trafalgar Square, and there were some clear instructions in that video. This is going to be a long week." DCI Ford walked to the nearby Sergeant, "No one gets near, and I want four armed guards here round the clock, get that perimeter back and no one speaks to the media yet. Let the CSI do their jobs, not that I expect them to find anything." He paused "This guy has a plan, he's thought this through."

"Yes, Sir," was the response from the Sergeant and he walked off with a purpose.

Ford walked towards two Detective Sergeants, one was on a phone but ended the call as Ford approached. "Is it real boss," he quizzed.

"That the wife Burnham?" Ford threw back at him, "Better tell her you're going to be busy this week." He glanced at the taller Detective. "No messing up on this one Ash, the gun is real, the video is real, the media is here and you better dam believe that we're being watched by everyone."

"What's the play boss?" Ash Chilton was the youngest of the three men, 35 and only four years a Detective Sergeant.

"Well this place is mobbed, we're heading back to the Yard, get me any and all footage of this square in the last twelve hours, I want a face. Get CSI on the video if they aren't already, I want to know when and where it was posted. The names, I want them at the Yard, individual rooms, I want them comfortable but treat them with ignorance until we know more. At 9pm that guy George might be sitting in that chair."

Ford, Burnham, and Chilton made their way to an unmarked BMW, avoiding the commotion of the media trying to get a statement. On the journey back to the Yard calls were made from their phones putting into action a plan for an event they had never even imagined, let alone planned for.

Monday, April 10th, 2016 5am

As Wendy came too, she felt like she was waking from a night of too much red wine. Her eyes opened and slowly focussed, and as they did dread filled her heart. The sight before her terrified her very soul. She tried to scream, but as she moved her mouth she gagged, realising that she had something shoved in there, a rag that was preventing her tongue from moving and was wrapped around her head tightly. She intended to remove it with her hands, but they were stuck, the shrill noise of metal on metal made her look down at her wrists, seeing them held in place by handcuffs only added to her fear.

What she had seen that had terrified her so much, was a woman on a hospital gurney, unconscious or dead she wasn't sure, gagged, and handcuffed to the handles with her hands down by her side. The chill of realisation made her muffle out a cry and tears streamed down her cheeks as she realised she was trapped; just like the woman she was looking at. Turning her wrists, she touched the cold metal frame of her gurney and wrapped her fingers inside the ring of the cuff attached to the bed frame. She pulled hard, hoping in vain that the cuffs would give way and allow her to escape from this terrible place.

The dread and fear were too much, she exploded in a frenzy of thrusts, unable to move her feet which were held in place by a Velcro strap, with another tightly across her chest. But it didn't stop her trying, screaming, crying. A frenzy that was halted as the dusky room was lit up by a TV in the corner, fastened to the wall on a bracket about six feet above the floor.

Wendy froze, sweat broke on her forehead and she watched the video, hearing Georges' name being readout. When the video ended the TV switched off. She moaned, and sobbed, lying loose on the gurney. After what felt like an eternity, she scanned her eyes around the rest of the room, craning her neck as much as she could. She could see seven gurneys, seven people lying in exactly the same trap she was in. On the gurney next to her, the woman began to stir. Instantly she caught Wendy's eye and they stared terrified at each other. After a few moments, the woman felt the gag in her mouth, her eyes welled up and she traced her vision up and down Wendy. As she did she tried to move her wrists, her body, her feet, and then began to sob as Wendy was.

The crying and sobbing were once again interrupted by the TV in the corner. The video played again. As the name Martin Imbeault was read out the woman screamed through her rag.

Wendy's empathy for the woman matched her own fear of where she was. She was a practical woman, although not particularly strong. At fifty-six years old she had never really been independent, but she had learned that if she wanted things done she would need to do them herself, George certainly didn't lend a hand. He earnt the money that was all he needed to do. She began to look around the room again, there must be something she can use to get off this foam mattress with its blue plastic cover.

The room had a relatively low ceiling, cables and pipes ran across the open beams. She was sure it was a basement, those were floorboards from the room above. It was dark but she could see light, it came from a tiny air brick, the kind with nine little holes in it. There was not much light but enough to see a door, not too far from her. It was metal and looked solid, she could see the frame of the door on this side, a bolt slid into a hole in the wall, the loop of the bolt through a hole in the door, presumably padlocked from the other side. As she scanned her eyes taking in as much as she could from her strapped position, she noticed some dark patches on the floor and against the wall. As she stared at them a shiver went through her body as she was sure they were dark red. Her thoughts racing through her mind, trying to convince herself that she was imagining the colour. There was nothing else in the room aside from the seven gurneys and their patients. The woman to her right was crying, as was she, when another patient began to wake up.

Monday, April 10th, 11am

In an interview room at the Yard, George was giving a statement to a Detective about the last twenty-four hours. Outside, Ford stood with Burnham and Chilton, he glanced through the narrow wired glassed window at a non-descript gentleman in his late fifties, sitting on a chair wondering what was happening to his wife.

"What do we know of the seven?" Ford turned back to his team.

"Well, this guy has a clean record, works at a printing press as a duty manager, married twenty-six years, 58 years old, no children, financially sound." As Chilton reeled off the obvious, he sensed Ford's impatience, "There have been a couple of calls to the property dating back ten years with regards to alleged domestic violence, but no charges have ever been landed."

Burnham chimed in "We have Constables canvassing the neighbours, might turn up a few stories. As for the others, nothing screams out as a connection between them." He thumbed open his note pad, "Nicola Johnston, single Mum, 38 is missing her 19-year-old son Chris, disappeared on his way back from night shift from a restaurant kitchen where he was a pot washer. Harry Singh, 40, missing his elderly Dad, seems he came home and he was just gone. The old guy suffers from early onset Alzheimer's. Then we have Claire Papadopoulos, the youngest of them, good looking girl, 36 years old, missing her boyfriend, Gregory, who works in a call centre, never came home from the gym last night." He flipped a page and glanced at Ford before carrying on after getting a slight nod from him "Martin Imbeault, missing his wife, Donna, this guy, 56, was working away when he came home to find his children at home but no wife. Roy Ritchie, 65 years old, missing his daughter, Michelle, 40, who recently moved back home after a failed marriage. And that just leaves Michael Wenham, 55, his partner David was supposed to pick him up from work last night, the last he heard was a text half an hour before." Burnham flipped the notebook closed.

"No apparent connection between them boss," explained Chilton, "we've checked the location and the home addresses work on pretty much a loop around south London, a route about ten miles in total, crossing two bridges. We're checking CCTV as we speak, we'll get a vehicle soon. All victims appear to have been abducted within a five-hour window, starting with George's wife Wendy in there," he nodded toward the room, "and we think all taken in the order that they are mentioned on the video, from what we can tell."

Ford glanced at his watch, it was nearly noon, nine hours to catch this guy. "What are CSI saying about the video?" he asked without turning his gaze from the side of George's head.

"Not much they can say so far," replied Chilton, it's almost impossible to trace the origin, the email address used to load the video to YouTube is linked to a random bunch of personal information, it's likely it was loaded from a burner, so the IP address goes nowhere. They are running traces to see if they can pinpoint where it was uploaded, maybe we can get a face for the media. Getting YouTube to close down the account is almost impossible but we're working on it, however, it's easy to set up another email address and load another video if he wants to. Plus the video has been shared millions of times already and it's all over the TV."

Ford turned to his Detectives "These could be completely random innocents, but I want everything uncovered, if they've got a skeleton it's time to open the cupboard." He pushed the handle down and entered the room.

The Sergeant at the table stopped writing and got up from the chair "That's all for now, thanks," Ford gestured the Sergeant to leave the room, his voice had changed, calming, considerate, "Mr. Russ, I'm DCI Ford, I'm so sorry to meet you under these circumstances." George nodded, his eyes were raw, he had been crying but those tears were dried now. In front of him was a coffee, George placed his hands around the cup and leaned forward.

"Where's my wife?" it was a simple question, but a difficult one to answer.

"Mr. Russ, I have fifty police officers working on this, we're doing everything we can to locate your wife. Any information you can give me, anything no matter how small or insignificant you think it is, you need to tell me as it will help. Tell me about your wife?" Ford pulled out a chair that scraped on the floor as he was speaking and sat down.

George took a sip from the coffee, now lukewarm. "I got home from work last night she wasn't in, I thought she was at her sisters' but she wasn't, figured she was in a huff with me."

"Why would she be in a huff?" Ford interjected, considering the timescale, he wasn't going to use his usual technique of tiring them out to get the information he wanted, and his instincts kicked in that something wasn't right about this man sat across from him.

"Oh, er, we had a row Saturday night, you know how women are…" George seemed unsettled by the way Ford was looking at him.

"No, not married, tell me."

"Well," George took another sip, "why is this relevant, us having a row isn't going to find Wendy, you could be out looking for her."

"I have a full team looking for her, I'm trying to find out why I am looking for her?"

"Because some crazy bastard has taken her for fuck sakes," George barked.

"But why her, what made him choose her," Fords voice was calm, undeterred by George's outburst.

"How the hell should I know," George stared at Ford, not sure what to make of him, but not liking the questions he was being asked, he felt nervous, leaning back in his chair and folding his arms, avoiding Ford's prying gaze.

Ford leaned in a little "Can you tell me about the police being called to the house Mr. Russ?"

"What the fuck has that got to do with it," he said surging forward from his reclined position, "I never did anything wrong and I was never charged with anything." George was defiant with his body language and tone when answering the questions.

As he sat back in his chair, Ford's tone of voice changed to one of almost idleness "Have you seen anyone hanging around the property lately?"

George shifted in his seat, ignorant now of the cold coffee "No, don't think so. I got a camera installed in the back garden, some kids got in and woke Wendy up, since then nothing."

"When did you get that installed?" Ford's interest was pricked.

"About three months ago, got it off Amazon, £100, big waste of money if you ask me, just Wendy hearing things, said she heard kids in the garden. Never caught anything on it." George sat still with his arms folded, this brief interview had felt like an interrogation.

"Do you know anyone called Malcolm?" Jim's question was short.

"Not that I know of," his gaze was now focussed on the table in front of him.

Jim scanned this man with his eyes, looking for a sign of weakness. He glanced at George's hands clasped around his coffee cup, spotting some yellowing around the first and second knuckle of his right hand. "Have you ever known anyone called Malcolm?"

The man with the bruised knuckles looked up at Jim, drawing in his breath, "Not for a long time."

"Tell me more," he took out his notepad ready to write down anything of interest, "Any detail could help."

"There was this little shit of a kid when Wendy and I used to foster," George folded his arms tighter than they already were, an involuntary act that peaked Jim's curiosity, "his name was Malcolm, about twenty years back I think, apart from that I can't think of anyone else called Malcolm that I know."

"Why did you stop fostering?" as Ford asked, he noticed George fidgeting, uncrossing his arms now and he ran his left hand over the knuckles of his right, an action the man didn't even realise he had made.

"It was Wendy who wanted to foster," George grunted, "she couldn't have kids, too much hassle if you ask me, looking after other people's little shits. During the nineties, it got too much like hard work, social services, paperwork, etc., so I made her give it up."

"Can you be more precise about this kid Malcolm? Do you remember when he stayed with you, a surname?" Jim opened his notepad.

George rolled his eyes, "Fuck, probably around 1990."

"Do you remember why he was staying with you?"

"God knows, we live in a nice neighbourhood, but we always got messed up kids from the estates," he shifted in his chair, "you know one of the little fuckers punched me once, and I got in trouble for defending myself."

"Is that right?" Ford's voice had a tone of sarcasm about it as he flipped his notebook closed.

"What happens now?" George spoke with a tone that implied impatience.

Ford was about to get to his feet, he paused "Well if I don't catch the fucker who has your wife before 9pm, I'll be asking you the same thing." His instincts were that he didn't like George, but he had a job to do and an innocent woman to save. "I'd like you to stay at the Yard, I might need to talk to you again." He paused as he was leaving the room "That looks like a fresh bruise on your knuckle Mr. Russ." George covered his hand as a child would cover a sweet they had taken without permission. Ford left the room.

As he walked along the corridor Ford reached for his phone and dialled Burnham "I want the other six questioned, this guy Russ is handy with his fists and he has guilt and fuckwit husband written all over him. He was in the fostering game back in the late eighties or early nineties, remembers a kid called Malcolm staying with them but can't remember why."

"I'll get onto social services boss, but that's a long while back," replied Burnham.

Monday, April 10th, 1pm

On his way up to the Super Intendant's office, Ford carried a cup of fresh hot black coffee. He chapped the door and entered. "Ma'am." He addressed Super Intendant MacHray. She sat behind her desk finishing a phone call, gestured to Ford to take a seat and hung up.

MacHray sat back in her leather desk chair "Well this is a shit storm for a Monday morning."

"We've had no leads, no links, a chair, a gun, seven missing and seven relatives, and a video that has been seen by everyone from the Pope to the Dalai Lama!" Ford and MacHray had been partners before her promotion, both as detectives and between the sheets. It had been pretty low key, with rumours and gossips filling in the blanks around the Yard. The physical connection between the two of them had lasted on and off for a few years but had developed into friendship over time. Alison was at the top of her game as a detective but had an additional skill of being able to manage the politics which had seen her rise to the big chair, a position that Jim truly believed she deserved and knew that she was extremely effective in.

"What's your play, Jim?" Between the two of them, in a closed office, they were informal. Ten years working together meant they had no secrets or reason to distrust.

"Oh fucked if I know Alison, I'm braving it out there, but my mind keeps expecting to see a man with a gun in his mouth at 9pm. I've got nothing, and yet I've got everyone working on it." He sighed and took a long swill of his coffee, piping hot but just the way he liked it.

"Tell me about the victims." Her role here was the coach, she didn't know what to do either, that was the problem with such a case, and there was no rule book.

"A varying bunch, wives, daughters, fathers, and the families that are here, regular Joes, nothing to make them stand out. I've just met Mr. Russ, he has a history of beating his wife, no charges but a fresh bruise on his knuckle. He's a fucking dinosaur. Used to foster kids, remembers one called Malcolm, it's loose but I've got Burnham looking into it. I got a hunch he wasn't exactly foster dad of the year either."

"Do you think he'd do it?" Alison asked the question bluntly, Ford raised his eyes to her, with a quizzical look, "well everyone is going to be asking it come 9pm Jim. This fucker who took his wife has set a challenge."

"Well they certainly aren't random people, he's planned it. The route, the timings, George mentioned he heard kids in his back garden, got himself some CCTV. Could have been him staking out the joint. I'm sure I'll hear similar things from the other six, but that only gives a pattern, not evidence." He took another big gulp, "we're looking for the pick-up vehicle, but this guy feels clever, it will only give make and model, fake plates guaranteed. The gun could come from anywhere, probably no prints on it, CSI say they won't be able to trace the video. Hopefully, we can narrow down where it was uploaded from, at least give me a search area." He had spoken like a politician, avoiding the question she had asked.

"I'll handle the media Jim, you've got a lot of work to do. What's your plans for 9pm," the way she looked at Ford was unflinching. But he knew what she meant, he wasn't going to find this woman before 9pm, and he then had to make a decision.

"Well." He sighed, "The gun is real and loaded, and the place is cordoned off up to 200 yards. The media are in full view along with a million bloody camera phones. If we haven't got her by 9pm, the choice is up to Mr. Russ, and then we'll find out how real this thing is." Saying it out loud was like lifting the weight of the world off his shoulders. He had been perusing that thought since 8am this morning, everyone was thinking it, "and if we don't catch Malcolm, it's only going to get worse."

"What do you need from me Jim," she understood the responsibility Ford had, her job was to make this as media-friendly as the circumstances allowed and cut out as much red tape as possible.

"Riot teams on standby, there were hundreds of people out there already this morning, it's going to be mayhem tonight. I'll get you a face and a vehicle as soon as possible, I want it on the news, and if I can get a grid to work in I want men going to door to door if needed. This guy has seven people trapped somewhere, someone must have seen something." With that, he stood up, took his coffee, and nodded before leaving her office.

Monday, April 10th, 3pm

"We've got a face," said Burnham, marching into the operations room, "and it worries me to fuck."

"Why, do we know him?" Ford was sat at a desk looking over the details of the families affected, trying to find a link.

"No, not yet, it's from Trafalgar Square, CCTV picked him up placing the chair and the gun at 7am this morning. It's not the face that worries me, boss, he stared into the camera. He's not hiding his face." Burnham threw the photo down on the desk. A man, mid-thirties, looked back up at Ford. Short hair, stubble, good looking. It wasn't a high definition picture, but it was enough for someone to recognise him.

Ford picked up the picture and stared at it as if he was staring at the man himself, a worrying chill went down his spine as Malcolm stared back. "Get it on the news, we had nothing but at least this will give us a million pairs of eyes looking for him. He must be known somewhere, he has to eat, a newsagent, a delivery boy, and someone knows where this man is. Take it to MacHray." Burnham shot out of the room. Ford picked up the phone and dialled MacHray. "Burnham is on the way up, we have a photo of the bastard, go public with that and man the phones."

"I'll be on air in 20 minutes, I was going empty-handed, at least I can give the vultures something," MacHray replied and hung up.

Chilton had been in conversation on a phone call at a desk in the corner of the room, he hung up and directed his attention to Ford. "Was that a pic of Malcolm?"

"Yup, MacHray is going live with it now. What have you got?" Ford turned in his chair to face Chilton.

"The people in the video, we've had detectives chatting to them all morning. Maybe we've got something. You spoke to Mr. Russ, bruised knuckles, a bit of a dinosaur you called him. Means it's a rocky relationship, and he's a coward." Chilton got up out of his seat and walked over to Ford's desk, perching on the edge. "Well Nicola Johnstone is missing her son, he's a 19-year-old lad. She was asked if anyone might have a vendetta against either of them. She broke down crying saying it might be her own brother. See, it turns out that her son Chris was accused of molesting the niece, the brother's seven-year-old daughter, some years back. Seems nothing came of it other than counselling and the usual social services involvement. But it's not the brother, he's at work with solid alibis. Then there is Harry Singh, a Sikh guy caring for his elderly Dad, what's more noble, right? But we have searched his house with a warrant in the last hour, he was refusing us entry. That call was from the detective at the property. In the old guys' bedroom, they found a pair of handcuffs attached to a radiator in what was described as a cesspool. Seems the devoting son has been claiming benefits, disability, driving in a new disabled car, lording it around like he's some kind of saint, all the while his father lives in squalor."

"Keep going," Ford knew Chilton well enough that his hunches usually amounted to something.

"And there is Claire Papadopoulos, she's been shagging her boyfriend's boss. Squealed like a pig when we told her we could access her texts, usual ruse. The boss has a rock-solid alibi but now might be getting a divorce. Martin Imbeault, two teenage children, we checked his file and he has a history of allegations regarding interactions at a youth centre and as a football coach, he no longer works there, but social services are talking to the children now, and I bet I know what they'll say. He's been asked to hang around like the rest of them." Chilton walked over to the water cooler, filled a cone and took a sip, holding his notebook in the same hand. "So far

I have nothing on Roy Ritchie and his missing daughter, or Michael Wenham and his boyfriend."

"So what you're saying is they are all assholes who deserve this?" Ford knew that wasn't the answer, but wanted Chilton to complete his theory.

"Boss, they are all guilty of something. Affairs, molesting children, cruelty … but they aren't the ones that were taken. The innocent ones were taking, the cheated boyfriend, the abused Dad, except the innocent mother who tried to protect her kid? … Wendy the abused wife. They are all innocent, and this guy Malcolm is testing the guilty ones. It's not perfect, but it's what I'm working with at the moment"

Chilton wheeled out a desk chair and sat down about six feet from Ford. He could see Ford was perusing his theory. "How does it help us find him," asked Ford.

Chilton sat, stone-faced, it was a good theory but a better question, he snorted out of his nose and he gulped down the rest of his water. "He must know them." He paused. Deep in thought looking down at the floor. "Seven people, in a small geographic area, all with something to hide, some pretty big secrets."

Ford piped up, "It's not seven yet till we fill in the blanks," he looked at the clock on the wall. "It doesn't matter just yet, shove the news on, and let's see how MacHray handles this." Chilton went over to a TV in the corner, flicked on BBC News and sat back down."

The news presenter interrupted a pundit who was giving his views on the validity of the video. MacHray appeared walking up to a press conference table.

"I'll be making a statement on the news story that has broken this morning. There will be no questions at this stage. At approximately 7am this morning a video was uploaded to YouTube detailing the abduction of seven members of the public. This statement was made by a man calling himself Malcolm. In the video, he states he has placed a chair with a revolver on it at Trafalgar Square. This I can confirm is true. He has also made demands for seven individuals to place the gun in their mouths and pull the trigger, one by one at 9pm every evening this week. We have now found these individuals and talking with them here at Scotland Yard. We can also confirm that they are all reporting the disappearance of someone close to them.

"On your screens now and being circulated to the media is a photo of the man we believe to be Malcolm along with a phone number to contact if you think you recognise him. No matter how insignificant you may think it is, we need to hear from you. If you see this man in the street, please do not approach him and he is to be considered armed and dangerous. If you see him dial 999 immediately.

"We have 50 officers assigned to this case and are currently facilitating a very large investigation to ascertain the whereabouts of these seven innocent civilians. We have armed officers at Trafalgar Square and we have left the chair and the gun untouched. There will be a large police presence around the Square until this situation is resolved and Malcolm is found.

"Until we have more information to give I will not be answering any questions." With that MacHray stood up from the desk and left the room as the media launched in a foray of questions and noise.

Back in the room, Ford turned to Chilton. "It's 3pm, in six hours we're going to see what Mr. Russ is made of."

January, 2016

As the pot boiled Wendy picked up the wooden spoon, turning the potatoes in an anti-clockwise direction. She cast her eye over to her magazine, licking the thumb of her right hand and flicking a page over. Considering whether she should cut out the coupon for the hair dye and dare to try a new brand, she grabbed the oven glove, placing it on her hand she opened the oven door and half withdrew the baking tray, checking the Frey Bentos pies, and then sliding them back in after deciding another ten minutes would be enough. Removing the glove and tossing it on her magazine, she walked out of the kitchen, opened the cupboard door under the stairs and lifted out the vacuum cleaner. Uncoiling the cable, she leaned down to the plug socket and plugged it in, flicking the switch and pressing her toe against the power button. Sliding the upright along the hallways she looked at her watch briefly. Perfect, George would be home in fifteen minutes, enough time to whiz the vacuum around and get his tea out.

After a quick dash around the living room, tidying the papers under the coffee table and plumping Georges cushion, she coiled the vacuum cable and returned it to the cupboard. Back into the kitchen she stirred the potatoes again and turned the dial on the microwave to three to heat his beans. She didn't like them nuked, but he wouldn't have them done in a pan so she got used to them that way. Opening the wall cupboard, she removed two plates and sat them on the side, and placed a wooden board alongside it for the baking tray. From a lower cupboard, she removed the metal colander and placed it in the sink.

Fixing the oven glove to her hand again she opened the oven door and began removing the pies. A clatter of what sounded like bottles from outside made her jump, and she lost her grip on the tray, causing the pies to fall on the floor, upside down. One of the pies spat boiling hot gravy up her shin which made her yelp out, but she froze looking at her reflection in the kitchen window.

"Hello," she called out. Her voice trembled as she stood perfectly still trying to hear any noises from beyond her own face staring back at her. She ignored the heat on her shin, and stepped towards the back door, reaching out for the key and turning it. Her palm was clammy as she turned the handle and slowly pulled the door towards her. "Hello?" She called a little louder into the darkness, and then remembered the light switch to her left. Flicking it on it took a second for the connection to reach the LED bulbs and illuminate the back patio. Peering out first she then plucked up the courage to step onto the terracotta slabs.

Looking around her garden she didn't see anything at first, but then she cast her eyes down. The red recycling box that was filled with glass bottles she had carefully washed and put outside, had moved a couple of inches, and two of the bottles were sitting on the floor beside it. She glanced back into the garden as scanned the bushes. "Get out of my garden you toerags," she shouted towards the back fence, "my husband will be home any second." She paused for a moment, steeling to hear any noise at all.

After deciding whoever it was had gone she turned and walked back in through the kitchen door, startled by her husband who was stood at the other side of the kitchen. She took a short breath, and turned, closing the door behind her. He stood staring at the pies, gravy seeping from one of them, on the tiled floor and sprayed up the door of one of the kitchen cupboards. "I'll put some more on George, they won't be long," she immediately bent down on her knees, picking up the foil cups and the metal tray, "there was someone in the garden, they startled me."

"You saw them?" George asked, looking towards the back door and back at her.

"They kicked over the bottle's box," she said, as she reached for her tea towel on the side and began wiping up the smashed pies. "I got a fright, George, that's all, probably kids."

"Probably?" George inflected his voice slightly, "so you didn't see anyone?"

Wendy continued to clean up the pies, her knees uncomfortable on the stone tiled flooring. She didn't look up at her husband, scooping the crusts onto the baking tray. "They were gone before I got out there."

George stood still, looking around the kitchen, surveying the mess. "So if you didn't see anyone, what happened to the bottle box?"

Wendy began to tremble. She took a deep breath. "There was a noise, I heard …"

George cut her off, "So if you didn't see anyone," his tone slowed, emphasising the word 'see', "what happened to the bottle box?"

She stopped moving, thinking about her words carefully, as she began to answer his big hand clamped down on the back of her neck, squeezing tight, pushing her face towards the floor. "What was in the garden, Wendy." He had always been strong and forceful with her, he shook her neck back and forth, making her head rock as she let out a whimper. "WHAT WAS IN THE GARDEN!!!"

She sobbed, "Nothing."

"WHAT!!" his voiced made her jump and wince.

"Nothing," she repeated as a tear ran down her cheek. He let go of her neck and stood up straight, taking a deep inhale of breath, and exhaled over a good few seconds. She did not move an inch.

In a swift strike he punched her in the side of her left temple, knocking her face into the floor, hitting the tiles hard, she let out and loud yelp as he connected. Her face, covered in pie, she placed her hand's palm down on the floor, trying to lift herself up, her head dazed and her vision blurred. As the second punch landed on the back of her head she went back down. This time she stayed lying with her body on the floor, her right leg stretched out, her left bent at the knee.

George stood up again, looked at his wife. "Fuck," he sighed, "I'm going to the chippy." With that he turned and headed back down the hallway and without hesitation opened the front door, slamming it behind him as he left.

Monday, April 10th, 9am

In the darkened room, the TV had now played seven times. Each patient was now awake, they had all screamed, thrust, cried, sobbed and heard their loved one's names on the screen as the video played. Some were still moaning, some continued to cry. The gags in each of them were tightly rigged, but none the less they were trying to make eye contact and talk to anyone in the room. Very little could be understood by any of them.

With a loud jolting scrape that echoed through the room, the bolt was slid to the left and the door opened. In walked a man, with a tray, loaded with bottles and straws, light from an upstairs bulb illuminating him. He wore simple blue jeans and a plain white t-shirt, it was tight revealing a toned physique. His appearance caused some screams, Wendy was the closest to the door, she was crying and trying to shift away from him without success. He walked to the corner of the room, there were some exposed breeze blocks on the corner that formed a ledge, he placed the tray down and picked up one of the bottles.

Walking towards Wendy he untwisted the cap, and she tried to back away again. He raised his finger "Shhh I am not going to hurt you" he said. The voice was kind. "If you hadn't already guessed, my name is Malcolm and you are my guests." He pushed the gag from her mouth and removed a bendy straw from his pocket. Placing it in the bottle he said: "drink, please."

Wendy was frozen but she needed to drink. She leaned her head as far forward as her restraints would allow and sipped from the straw. Malcolm was staring at his other guests as she drank. "You will all be looked after during your stay, I will not harm any of you as long as your loved ones do the right thing." He looked down at Wendy, her eyes were red raw with tears, "Everyone please meet Wendy. Your husband is up first, its 9am, tonight he'll be sitting in the seat. One way or another he will never hit you again. I'll be back at five past nine tonight once we see how he gets on." He gestured to the TV on the wall.

He replaced the gag and put the lid back on the bottle after discarding the straw in a trash bin sitting just inside the entrance. He walked back over to the tray, picked up a second bottle and moved to a boy nearest Wendy. He was shaking with fear as Malcolm removed the gag, opened a bottle, and inserted a straw. "P... P...Please let me go," he whimpered. He raised his finger to his lips.

"Drink, you'll be here until tomorrow," he said with a monotone voice, he leaned his head forward and drank as Wendy had done, "This is Chris, everyone, he's 19. He has been a very naughty boy. Five years ago you played around with your little cousin, and it went further than doctors and nurses, didn't it? Your mother was devastated, she did the right thing and got social services involved, you spent a little bit of time in care, but it ripped her family apart. She doesn't speak to her brother anymore and has been shunned by her other siblings and her mother. She cares for you, she loves you, but she is tired. I wonder what she'll do tomorrow night." Chris began to scream, and thrash around in the bed, Malcolm calmly pushed the gag back into his mouth. "Shhh Chris, it might just work out ok."

Taking another bottle of water he moved to a gurney with an elderly man, the same routine as before but the man was solid, he didn't flinch as he drank from the straw, "Mr. Kalarahi, how are you today? Everyone, this is Mr. Kalarahi and I have to offer a sincere apology to him. You see this man is 75 and he suffers from Alzheimer's, his son, who is supposed to love him and care for him, keeps him handcuffed to a radiator while he spends all of his money. I am very sorry for having you strapped to this bed, but it is very necessary." Mr. Kalarahi glared at Malcolm without saying a word, he was in a lucid state, and he knew what was going on as Malcolm returned the gag to his mouth.

"Oh Gregory, you must be very confused," He said as he removed the gag from the next man. This guy was tall, strong, and he was not very happy to be strapped to the gurney is this basement.

"I'm gonna fucking kill you, you fucking cock sucker!" he screamed at Malcolm, spitting in his direction. "Get me off of this fucking bed and I'll shove that bottle of fucking water up your fucking arse." Malcolm removed the straw from the bottle and screwed the lid shut. Gregory was trying with all his strength to loosen the restraints without success.

"Uh, uh, you don't get a drink for that Gregory," Malcolm forced the gag back into his mouth, it was difficult as Gregory was rocking his head from side to side. He was screaming through the gag, the veins on the side of his forehead bulged, his fists were clenched. He was making quite a noise as the handcuffs clanked against the frame of the gurney. "You see Gregory, you are innocent, but your girlfriend, Claire, and your boss, well they've been doing the fandango while you've been working on those fabulous muscles of yours." Gregory froze for a moment to consider what he had just heard, then decided it enraged him even more so returned to the futile thrashing about. "When you've accepted that you can't get yourself free and you've calmed down, I'll return with your water."

Moving for another bottle he approached Donna, a woman lying quite still on her gurney. Malcolm removed the gag. "I know why I'm here," she said immediately, with a calm voice, "and you're wrong, they were all wrong, Martin didn't do anything."

"Oh … you were meant to wait for me to introduce you Donna but seeing as you have this all figured out I'll let you explain why to your fellow roomies why you're here." Malcolm leaned against the bare brick wall, gesturing his hand to the group allowing her to begin.

"Martin was accused, that's what I'm hearing in this room, they all have secrets, they've all done wrong, but not my Martin, he was never charged, no evidence, he's innocent." With that statement, Donna lay straight back on her bed, looking straight up at the ceiling.

"Of course he is, but you made a mistake in what you said there. There wasn't enough evidence, it's a critical word that means so much." Malcolm stood upright again, unscrewing the cap from the water bottle, and then leaned toward her face, so he was about a foot away. "You see, Martin was clever, he'd make his kids feel special and then scare the shit out of them so they'd never say anything. They were terrified to go to football practice. You see, Martin is what, 56? I'm 38. That means when he made me put my hand inside his shorts he was only 30. I was terrified, and I never went back to football." Donna froze, staring into his eyes, a tear escaped from her eye and ran down her cheek towards her ear. He began to walk around the room, "I could have been David Beckham for all I know, but Martin took that from me. I was weak though, I should have said something and maybe all those other children could have grown up to be whatever they dreamed. But I have made my peace with that, I was a child, and I was abused." He returned to Donna, let her sip from the straw, she never said anything else, and he replaced the gag.

Of the two remaining patients, a man and a woman, he approached the woman first. Once she was sipping her drink he started speaking. "Michelle Ritchie, lovely to meet you. You are an exception to everyone else here as far as I can tell. You are an only child, recently separated but that's not uncommon, you have no children and have moved back to stay with your widowed father." He began to speak to the rest of the room. "You see, every good experiment needs a control subject. If you hadn't worked it out by now, following Donna's outburst, you are all here because either you or your loved one has been very, very immoral. But not Michelle and her Dad. You see, Michelle, although she is separated, worked hard on her marriage, as did her husband. Counselling, holidays etcetera, and now they have split they are even on good speaking terms. An amicable break shall we call it." Malcolm's voice was almost preaching to the group now, like this was the pinnacle of his plan. "Your Dad cared deeply for your Mother when she was ill with cancer, and when she died two years ago, he grieved appropriately. He was there for you when you separated, and even then he tried to help the two of you out by paying for your trip to New York. That is love people."

He walked back to Michelle, looked at her kindly "Unfortunately, to prove my point this week, one of you will need to die." With that Michelle began to scream, Malcolm forced the gag back into her mouth and her muffled screams slowly waivered into a whimper. She was still sobbing when Malcolm approached the last patient, a man around the age of fifty-five, well dressed in an expensive suit.

"David, hello, how are you?" Malcolm asked as the straw entered his mouth.

"What do you want, why am I here," David asked, sucking down the water to quench his thirst.

"You don't know? Haven't you guessed yet?" Malcolm smirked at David, "I actually think you are my prize possession. Two people so immoral but so good at it they have been able to go unnoticed for years. What's the name of the Charity that you and your boyfriend Michael set up? Go on, tell the folks."

"What? What has that got to do with anything?" David's face was unsettled, his voice quivered.

"The Samuel Higgins Trust," Malcolm answered his own question. "You see people, David, and his boyfriend Michael here set up a charity after a local boy died of a rare form of cancer about twenty-five years ago. Since then they have been the toast of the town, invited to every glitzy award ceremony, paraded as the saviours they are, hell, David here even ran as an Olympic torchbearer. However," Malcolm had his finger pointed in the air to accent his point, "would you like to tell your roomies just how much of the money raised goes to anyone in actual need?" He glanced over at David, "No, oh that's good because I wanted that pleasure … just thirty-five percent people, thirty-five percent!! Which is strange because the Samuel Higgins Trust netted over £7.5 million last year through generous donations, and the operating profit from that was just ten percent. So for those that aren't good at quick arithmetic means £4,125.000 went into the back pockets of David and Michael." Catching a glance over at David again. "Nice suit."

After returning David's gag to his mouth he then returned to the tray in the corner, placing down the bottle and picking up the tray. "Oh, and David, the reason I know so much about the Samuel Higgins Trust, Samuel Higgins was my best friend, and when you two set up the charity it made me happy, so happy that two local strangers wanted to help and honour his memory."

He walked towards the door and placed the tray on one of the steps leading upstairs. He turned to face the room again, "Don't worry Wendy," he said, "I'll put the TV on so you can see what is happening and I'll be in just after nine." With that, he closed the door and slid the bolt back into the wall.

Monday, 10th April, 8pm

"Ford its 8pm, anything?" MacHray asked over the phone. Ford was waiting outside the break room where they had put Mr. Russ. With its couch and coffee machine, it seemed a little more comfortable than the interview room he had sat in most of the day.

"Just the same theory that Chilton has. He's digging into the family's backgrounds and we have them all being interviewed. Burnham is tracing CCTV cameras across the bridges hoping to find a vehicle." His voice was heavy, he was in a position he did not want to be in. "I'm going to ask Mr. Russ to make a choice. He can sit here and see what happens, maybe this is a bluff, or we can take him to the chair."

"Jim, we can't be seen to be giving into this guy, its insanity." Her voice inflected at the end, she wasn't even sure what should be done, but she just knew she didn't want to see a man blow his brains out on national TV.

"What's our options, Alison? We have very little today. This guy has a plan that is unfolding and we haven't been quick enough to stop act one. Mr. Russ pulls the trigger or at some point, we'll find Mrs. Russ' corpse, I have no doubt of that." He glanced into the room through the glass pane, George was sitting hunched forward on a couch, a brown plastic cup of coffee in his hands, staring down at the floor.

"The Media will crucify us, Jim." It was not an accusation, but a statement of fact. "I'll keep them off you and take the heat, you just keep me informed of every little detail. Jim," she paused before her next words, ensuring they were the right ones to say, "take him to the square if he wants to go. I have the riot teams already in place, Trafalgar Square is a circus right now. Med crews are down there as well."

Ford sighed, "When I woke up this morning I did not think I would be asking a man if he wanted to kill himself with a Revolver."

"Call me after nine, Jim." MacHray hung up.

As he pushed the door open, George jumped a little and looked up at Jim. "It's 8.15 George," Ford advised, "We haven't found her."

"What do we do now?" asked George, with a voice that sounded like Jim would offer a hopeful solution.

"Well George, the choice is yours I suppose." Ford pulled up a chair from the table in the corner and sat down facing George. "I can't find your wife in time, and you need to decide if you believe Malcolm and if your wife is in actual danger. It's a decision you need to make on your own, but if it is all true, and this sick game is all real, your wife needs saving."

George looked up at Ford, "What would you do?" He asked with a tear forming in the corner of his eye.

"I'm not married, George, and I can't answer your question for you. But I suppose you need to ask yourself if you love your wife, if you regret the beatings you've given her, the apologies that went nowhere, the fear that you imposed on her throughout your marriage." George made an attempt to protest, "Shut it, this is not pretend George. You know what kind of husband you've been, whether you admit to me or not I don't care, because in less than an hour either you or your wife will be dead, that I am sure of. And I know who I'd rather see walking the streets. The question is, after all the torment, are you going to be a man, or are you going to live like a pussy for the rest of your life and let your wife make the ultimate sacrifice."

George looked back down at the floor. He didn't say anything, he couldn't, everything DCI Ford had said was true, he was a shit husband, he was a bully, but there was no way he was admitting that to anyone.

"It only takes five minutes to drive to Trafalgar, but you have to make a decision, so I'll wait outside this room," glancing down at his watch, Ford added, "you only have ten minutes to make that decision, I'll be outside, if you open the door then we need to be quick to make it by nine." With that Ford left the room, closing the door behind him. Once outside he dialled a number, "make sure the roads are clear, we should be down in a minute."

Monday, April 10th, 8.45pm

A convoy of marked and unmarked police cars drove through the handful of streets that connected Scotland Yard and the square. Trafalgar square was busy, thousands of people were around the perimeter, and the media were up high on scaffolding, there were even a couple of Electric Scissor Lifts fifty feet in the air with cameramen on top. "Hmm, get a good view from up there," Ford thought to himself. He looked over his shoulder at George sitting in the back seat, he was looking down again, deep in thought.

As they pulled up, the whole of the square had been emptied, the police had cordoned off the perimeter with metal railings and officers were stood facing out at the crowd at about six-foot intervals. Ford climbed out of the car, he was surprised by the level of quiet amongst the crowd. He smirked inwardly as he thought this was what he imagined a modern-day execution would be like from medieval times, then checked himself for having a moment of levity. He walked round to the back door and opened it, George stepped out slowly, casting his eyes around the scene for the first time. He stopped as he set his eyes on the chair, about fifty yards away, sitting there menacingly on the grey slabs.

"I can't do it, Jim," he stuttered.

"You don't have to, George," Jim placed his arm around Georges' shoulder and leaned in, "It's you or her, you make the decision." George stood up as Jim looked at his watch, "it's 8.55 George, and you'll hear the chime of Big Ben. It's up to you now."

George walked round to the front of the car. He had never been a brave man, and he had not lived a life he had been proud of. He knew he was guilty, there was no one to lie to inside his own head, but he wrestled with his dilemma as he began walking to the chair. Each step was heavy, his thoughts drowned out the noise from the crowd. He didn't love his wife, she irritated him, she wasn't good looking anymore, she'd put weight on, she did nothing to lose the weight, he didn't like his boss, his work was boring, and he hit her when he was in a bad mood, and it wasn't just with his fists, he hit her soul with his tormenting. It was a long walk, he still hadn't decided what he was going to do. He tried to think at a million miles an hour about all the possible connotations that might happen in the next few minutes. What would people think if he didn't do it? Did he care? But then this could be a way out, did he need to keep going on? He found himself at the chair, he stared down at the revolver and then looked around at the crowd. They were eerily still and quiet, waiting for the outcome, watching like hyenas watch lions who pull apart a carcass, waiting to see what happened. He leaned down to pick up the gun, it was heavy, and the first time he'd ever lifted a gun. He examined it, turned it over, and sat down on the chair. Hunched forward, he felt a surging remorse for the pain he had inflicted on Wendy, she doted on him, always had his dinner ready, his clothes ironed, and she didn't ask for much. He was a bully, he'd spent his life tormenting her. She needed to be happy. She'd be happy without him. As the first chime rang out across London, George raised his trembling hand to his mouth and placed his lips around the end of the barrel. The second chime, third, he could do the right thing for once, forth chime, fifth, he was guilty, he was a pathetic man, sixth, seventh, but he was scared, he didn't want to die, eight … he dropped the gun from his mouth and burst out crying, wailing, sobbing like the broken man he was. As the ninth chime rang out Ford and several other officers were running in from the perimeter as George collapsed to his knees, the gun discarded on the ground.

June, 1986

George fumbled around the kitchen cupboard, sliding tins around and lifting packets of pasta front left to right. "Where the fuck are they?" He mumbled to himself, closing the cupboard door and opening the one next to it, sliding the contents back and forth. "Wendy where the fuck are they?" he hollered to his wife Wendy who was sitting through in the living room.

"What are you looking for?" Wendy replied, not moving from her couch or turning her gaze away from The Price Is Right.

He walked from the kitchen to the doorway looking into the living room, leaning on the doorframe. "My McCoys, Wendy, where are they?" He was looking directly at her as she sat on the couch, she turned her head away from the TV to look at him.

"I don't know babes, I haven't seen them." She uttered, not shifting her gaze from him.

Over his shoulder, George saw something move on the stairs, "Get down here now, both of you." His voice was firm, but not quite shouting. Malcolm and Isabella were sitting huddled together on the top step, and as George made his command the little girl squeezed into her big brother.

Wendy stood up from her couch, "George, let me.."

"Shut up!" He looked at her with serious eyes, and then back to the stairs, "Count of three, get down here." Again, not quite shouting.

The two young children slowly got to their feet and began descending the stairs, Isabella clutching tightly to her brother's arm. As they reached the bottom step and turned the bannister to face George, she buried her head into her brother's body and squeezed her eyes closed. Malcolm looked down at the floor. "Did you eat them?" His question was direct, Wendy stood just inside the living room, and she didn't want to move as she knew how George could be.

"No, sir," uttered Malcolm.

"Don't fucking lie to me boy," the raised voice of George made Malcolm flinch.

"George, he's eight," Wendy snapped and pushed past her husband, stepping in front of the two children. She turned towards George whose eyes showed he was clearly angry. "Let me handle this." George didn't move or alter his gaze. Wendy turned to the two children, Isabella still hiding her face in her brother's pyjamas. Her tone was soft and gentle, "Malcolm, you can be honest with me and not be scared. If you ate them please tell me, I can replace them, but we don't like liars in this house."

Malcolm raised his eyes to look at the woman who had been looking after them. "I ate them," he whispered, "but my sister didn't."

"Oh that's fine Malcolm, I'll go and get some more," she placed her hand on the side of his face, "if you are ever hungry while you're staying with us you need to come and tell me, not just take what you see."

"I'm sorry Wendy," Malcolm said, bowing his head briefly, he then looked over her shoulder at the angry man behind him, "I'm sorry Mr. Russ." He got no reaction from George, he stood and stared at the little boy briefly before walking into the living room without saying anything.

"Now it's late," Wendy said, "you two get to bed and settle in, I'll nip to the shop." With that Malcolm took Isabella by the hand and led her upstairs. Wendy picked up her coat from the peg in the hallway and fished her car keys out of the bowl. Calling towards the living room she asked, "Is there anything else you would like while I'm out?" She stood for a moment with no reply, "I'll be back soon then." With that, she opened the front door and headed to the shops.

After about half an hour she returned, a carrier bag in hand with a multipack of McCoys and a few other snacks, "I've got you a few bits and bobs," she said as she placed the keys in the bowl and removed her coat, returning it to the peg. She walked into the living room, placing the carrier bag on the coffee table, removing the crisps. "There, got you these, and some peanuts." Reaching back into the bag and removing her token offering of peace, giving them to George as he sat staring at the TV.

"How long are those brats going to be here?" He asked, not looking at his wife.

Wendy felt tense very quickly, she knew the mood her husband was in and she knew she needed to negotiate this situation carefully. Sitting down on the edge of the couch, facing George, she thought she should try and calm him down. "George babes, they've been through a rough time, they need a happy home while their Mum gets well." She was getting nothing from him, the cold stare he had was fixed on the TV. "Come on, George, even you said you wanted to do this." Still nothing from him.

"Phone the Social tomorrow and get them relocated," he was cold with his tone, "I'm not having junky thieves in my home."

"George!" she snapped at him and instantly regretted it.

He snapped his head towards her, "What? You wanted to take on every little scummy shit just to make up for the fact your tubes are fucked." Wendy's eyes welled up instantly. All she had ever wanted was to be a mother, and finding out she couldn't be one was the deepest pain she had ever felt. Being accepted for fostering had allowed her to feel some sort of bond with children which had dulled the pain. George had always supported it, until the first children had arrived, and he had instantly made his resentment clear.

"George that's cruel," she replied, trying to hold the tears back.

"You really think that's cruel?" he raised his voice, getting to his feet, looking down at her. She was looking up at him. "You really think that's cruel?!" He shouted even louder as he raised his hand and brought the palm down on her soft cheek. The slap was loud, knocking her off the edge of the couch into the gap between it and the coffee table. She squealed as she was struck, and George attacked again with speed. As she lay slumped he leant over her, making a fist and punching her in the back of the head, before getting back to his feet, panting with the exertion of the attack. He pulled his right foot back and kicked her twice in the back of the thighs as she lay, trying to curl up in a ball. "Get fucking rid of them little shits!" His voice screamed. Catching his breath, he left the front room, grabbing his coat from the hallway and headed out of the front door.

Malcolm lay in his bed, Isabella in beside him. They had heard the shouting which had frightened both of them. Isabella had run from her bed, jumping in beside her brother, and both of them now lay listening to Wendy crying in the front room after hearing the slam of the front door.

Monday, April 10th, 9.05pm

Wendy was crying as she watched George on his knees on the screen hanging on the wall. As he was rushed away by the police the TV switched off. She was groaning, "No, no, no" through her gag, as others in the room began to cry and some attempted to shout out. From the edge of the door, Wendy saw the light switch on. Footsteps on the stairs, the slide of the bolt and the door opened.

Malcolm entered the room, a carving knife in his hand. He walked up to Wendy, lying strapped to her gurney. Tears were streaming down her cheeks. "Wendy your suffering is almost over, your pathetic husband has chosen his life over yours. I am very, very sorry, but for the record, you were a very good foster mother." Her red eyes looked at Malcolm, a realisation of who this man was flashed through her mind. He placed his left hand on her chest as she attempted to throw her body into convulsions only for them to be impeded by the strong Velcro straps, with his right hand he slit her throat with the knife.

The residents of the room were all screaming through their gags, man and woman alike, blood sprayed up the front of Malcolm's white T-shirt. It sprayed for thirty seconds and Wendy gargled, a sickening, choking sound, blood covered the blue mattress, and spilled onto the floor. Malcolm stood back watching the life pour out of Wendy, her eyes fixed on his as they lost their light and her breathing stopped. The whimpers filled the room from the other guests. Malcolm said nothing. He began unstrapping her restraints, dug in his pocket for a key and unfastened the handcuffs. He undid the brakes with his foot and wheeled the gurney over to the wall. Lifting up the body in his arms, he flung her over his shoulder, blood soaking his jeans and shirt, dripping onto his boots. He left the room, the door wide open and mounted the stairs. A minute later he returned, pulled the door closed and locked it again.

Monday, April 10th, 11pm

Sitting in his office, Ford sipped at a coffee. When his phone rang he already sensed what it would be. He looked at the screen showing BURNHAM, "Is it her?"

"Yes, boss. Throat cut. She was found wrapped in a polythene sheet on a footpath on a quiet street. Forensics are here, we can expect the media anytime." Burnham said bluntly.

"Any witnesses?" Ford knew the answer.

"Not yet, boss, I've got men going door to door. We're checking local shop fronts round the corner for any sign of CCTV. Once everything is set up here, I'll head back in." The call disconnected. Ford was back in the break room, he'd have to go and tell Mr. Russ soon. He looked back at his phone, scrolled down and dialled MacHray, it was answered almost instantly.

"It's her, not formally ID'd but it's her. Throat cut, wrapped and dumped in plain sight." He stood up, picking up his coffee with his free hand. "Burnham is managing the scene, I'll go tell Mr. Russ."

"You ok Jim? That was tough tonight." MacHray was at home, but with a case like this, she was always working.

"Nothing else we could have done boss. I'll tell Mr. Russ and then I'll get some sleep. This all starts again tomorrow. At least we know Malcolm isn't bluffing."

"Get some sleep, Jim. I'll hold a press conference at 8am, update me at 7." She hung up.

He walked out of the room and headed to the lounge. As he entered, George was pacing up and down, his face looked angry, maybe at his own choices, or at his predicament, Ford didn't really care, his part of the game was over. "We've found a body we believe to be Wendy, Mr. Russ." He said it bluntly, he did not care for this man or his remorse, and the guy didn't deserve to feel bad. "We have forensics at the site, we'll bring her body to the morgue tonight and then we'll need you to formally identify her. Once you've done that you can go home." George stood and burst into tears, slumping down onto the couch after a few seconds.

Ford was not tolerating this and left the room, leaving George to wallow in his own misery, nodding to the police constable outside the room to look after him. He phoned Chilton. He answered quickly "How are you getting on with leads?"

"Head down to the ops room, I've set up a board, its taking shape. You ok boss?" Chilton asked knowing Ford had been through emotional turmoil.

"I'm good, George will be free to go home after he ID's the body, I'll be down in ten minutes." He stopped briefly on his way for a re-fill of coffee, saying hello to the occasional officer he passed, some he knew, some knew him. He thought about the week ahead, six more people were out there somewhere, this thing was only going to get worse unless he could catch a break.

As he entered the ops room the TV was on mute in the corner. The headline read that a body, thought to be that of Wendy Russ, had been found. The camera was a static image from the end of the street where her body was found. Tents had been erected and officers stood at each end of the street. Men in white overalls could be seen walking in and out of the tents, and at that moment men in black trousers and jackets wheeled a trolley into the back on a black private ambulance, on it a body bag. Ford stopped to watch for a second and then turned to Chilton who was busy building a board filled with photos, a map, red string and various pieces of information.

"So what have we got?" Asked Ford, perching on a desk.

Chilton walked to his board, "we know the route and have the vehicle, just confirmed in the last half an hour. It appears to be a white Mercedes Box van, approximately fifteen years old. The plates match a Fiesta registered in Manchester. Nothing too distinctive about it from what we can tell, but in these screenshots," he pointed to the top left of the board, "you can clearly see Malcolm, so he's not shy." He moved over to the right of the board. "Timings of the snatchings from 8pm to midnight confirmed in the order that Malcolm posted the names. In the middle here is the route, the cameras we got from either end of these two bridges across the Thames. Then we have the victims. I have four of them linked to Social Services cases over the past fifteen years at some point or other. It seems that our friends down at social services visited Wendy and George Russ five times over the last ten years. Nicola Alexander's son was referred for fostering for twelve months following the alleged assault on his cousin. He's in the system for that but according to his social work LAC reviews his behaviour was always a concern, a child that's possibly your worst nightmare." He took a gulp of cold coffee and winced as cold liquid hit his lips, Ford offered him his, he hadn't touched it, and Chilton took it without hesitation and took a sip. "We then move onto Martin Imbeault. Historical allegations of sex abuse of minors but no convictions, he's not worked at the youth centre or as a football coach for five years, but our reports have repeated calls to his property to investigate attacks on Martin from vigilantes, everything from smashed windows to him being attacked by a group in his own front garden. No charges have ever been filed on anyone related to assaults as Martin doesn't give us anything to go on. This case smells like a historical offender that we've not been able to nail to the cross. Over here we have Michael Wenham and his partner David Sutherland. Pillars of their community, fundraisers after setting up the Samuel Higgins Trust."

"Why do I know that name?" asked Ford, soaking up all of the information.

"Twenty-five years ago, the little lad who died of a rare form of cancer, got the media all over it as he was a huge Tottenham Fan and got to play on the pitch." Chilton looked for recognition, Ford nodded. "Well I was chatting to Michael myself, he's well-groomed, expensive suits, drove here in a Bentley. He's a charity fundraiser whose sole job is this Trust, smells like shit to me." Ford acknowledged an interest.

Chilton went and sat on a desk chair, using his feet to gently swing back and forward. "We've already agreed that Mr. Kalarahi is scum, but I have nothing on Roy Ritchie, in fact speaking to his neighbours and his daughter's ex-husband, the guy really sounds like a saint. His ex-son-in-law told us he was very supportive during the breakup and that they are all still very amicable. I'm still digging. And then the blonde bombshell, Claire Papadopoulos. Greek heritage, beautiful girl, shagging her boyfriend's boss every chance she gets."

"So, we have …" Ford paused, "had George and Wendy known to social services for an abusive marriage. Nicola Alexander and her son Chris, known to social services as he was a young teenager who abused a younger child. Nicola protects her son but he doesn't learn and continues to be a problem child." Ford traced his eyes over the board, putting the pieces of the puzzle together. "Harry Singh abuses his Dad and lives off the financial benefits, known to social services but allowed the poor old guy to live in squalor. Martin Imbeault abuses children whilst under his care and gets away with it, known to social services. If we dig, the other three are linked as well. The rich guys, get into their finances, you'll find something, the catalogue couple, speak to friends, if there are rumours you'll find them, and the perfect Dad, keep digging on him." Chilton smiled for the first time today. "What are you grinning for?" Ford snapped.

"You see boss," Chilton stood up looking at the board, "it's simple. This case isn't just aimed at them. It's us as well. Almost all of these people have been known to the police and or social services and nothing has helped them. This guy Malcolm is judge, jury, and executioner, whether he pulls the trigger or not, he wants the world to know these people have secrets." He turned to Ford.

"It's a theory, and a pretty dam good one." Ford, stood up to leave the room. He stopped, and turned back to Chilton, "We need to find him, and we need to know how he knows all of these people. Get onto Social Services first thing, we're looking for employees or ex-employees. Male, white, 30 to 40. Anyone that might have had access to these individual cases. Get Burnham on the rich couple and send him to blondie's work, he already has the link in with the family. I'll be here at 6 but I need to get some sleep, I'll be in my office if you need me." As he glanced down at the TV he looked back, "oh, and get on the phone to the morgue, I want Wendy's body prepped for viewing ASAP, get one of the constables to take that prick George to see his wife. I want her ID'd so that MacHray can face the vultures in the morning. See you at 8." With that, he left the room.

Tuesday, April 11th, 7.10am

The knock at the door stirred his sleep, "Boss you gotta see this," Burnham had opened the door, the bright light from the station corridor splintered into the office where Ford had been sleeping in his chair.

"What time is it?" Ford asked without opening his eyes.

"Ten past seven boss, your days going to be a long one," Burnham had walked in and placed a hot coffee on Ford's desk. He placed an iPad next to it, upright in its folding case, and pressed play on a video.

"Morning Britain. Last night act one completed, unfortunately with the loss of Wendy Russ, the loving and doting housewife of Mr. George Russ," it was Malcolm's voice, "twenty-five years married, no children. During their twenty-five years together, George had systematically beaten his wife and subjected her to verbal and mental torture. Their case was known to the Social Services and the police visited their home on multiple occasions, but he was allowed to go on abusing her. I have seen this with my own eyes."

The video had been of a fuzzy background, with Malcolm providing a voice-over. It cut to another video, the image was through a window, it was not great quality, but the 30 seconds of footage clearly showed George punching his wife Wendy while she was cowering on the floor. The image was stilled on George's grinning face, it was clear and unmistakably him. With the image still paused Malcolm continued to talk.

"Last night I gave George a chance to end her suffering by taking his own life, but by his cowardly action in Trafalgar Square last night, he has done just that was Wendy is no longer with us. George Russ lives at 14 Hempstead Road for those of you who didn't pay attention to my first video. Have a happy life, George."

The video ended. By now Ford was bolt upright. "When did this go up?"

"About 20 minutes ago Jim," Burnham replied.

"Where's Mr. Russ?" the urgency in Fords question sunk into Burnham quickly.

"He ID'd the body about 5am, a squad car dropped him off." Burnham was off out the door, "I'm en-route, get boys down there." He shouted as Ford fumbled for his phone. He called the despatch controller and sent cars to meet Burnham. His next call was to MacHray.

"Fuck Alison," he gasped, "this psycho is getting worse. MacHray had just seen the video herself.

"I'm calling in overtime, how many more men do you need?"

"All of them boss, and you've got to go and speak to the media, there's going to be a lynch mob outside Russ' house, I've got Burnham and a team heading there now." This was one hell of a way to wake up, Ford gulped the coffee, it burned his throat but at least he knew he was awake. "I want to cut as much red tape as possible on this one Alison, I'm taking them all into a room to read them the riot act, I want to know why these people."

"Whatever you need Jim, it's yours. I need to go speak to my superiors, then I need to brush my hair, if I'm going to look incompetent on national TV then I want to look good doing it." She hung up.

Ford hurried down to the ops room where a dozen officers were all busy doing something, "Give me good news about that video Chilton." Chilton was finishing a phone call and the poor sod didn't look like he'd had any sleep. As he hung up he shook his head.

"That was tech, same story, they are going to keep working on it, but these videos are almost impossible to trace. They are going to run forensics over the audio to see if it comes up with anything, but this guy can load as many as he wants, and we may never be able to trace him."

"Fuck," Ford finished his coffee, "is there any good news?"

"Well yes, I think so, a friend of mine in financial crimes had a look at the husband and husband team. Companies House has the Trust they set up running a turnover of seven mil, but only just over three mil goes to any good causes, he's picking up the detail, but I think that's their reason for being mixed up in this."

"Ok, you bring him in and grill him, maybe we'll get the answer out of him before your pal. What else you got, your grinning?" Ford looked him up and down, he was positively bouncing.

"Well that's the big news, I think I have Malcolm." Chilton had a grin like a schoolboy with his first crush.

"And you didn't start with that? Spill" Ford placed his mug on Chilton's desk.

"We've spent the night down at social services going through employee records and it turned up very little, but we had a call into the hotline from an anonymous woman who gave us a surname." He picked up a piece of paper and walked over to his case board, stabbed a pin in the paper centering it right in the middle of the map that formed the centre piece. He picked up a black marker pen and wrote MALCOLM POVEY. "We checked employee records, and it came up with nothing, then we checked sub-contractors. He was a cleaner for Sireon, a contractor for the council. His record show he was dismissed eighteen months ago. No longer lives at his last known address"

Ford smiled for the first time that morning. "It's definitely him?" Chilton picked up another piece of paper with the employee ID on it and stabbed next to the name he had written. Ford peered in. "Perfect." He picked up his phone and dialled his boss.

"Ma'am," conscious that Chilton was listening, he remained professional, "Chilton's got you a name. Malcolm Povey. Ex-cleaner for Sireon, worked at the local council officers, potentially had access to all cases involved."

"I'll put the name out there, Jim, thanks, turn the news on I'm on in ten minutes. Prepare to watch me get my ass kicked, but that name might help." She hung up. Ford turned the volume up on the news, the press conference was going live again. He turned to Chilton.

"Burnham is going to make sure Mr. Russ is safe, we'll probably have to give him security till this is over. Once he's checked that out, get him over to the bombshell's office, start digging around about her." Chilton was nodding his agreement. "I want you down at his old address and speaking to work colleagues who may remember him. I want some information on Malcolm, where did he hang out, properties he owns, anything. I'm going to take the remaining six and have a word with them all."

Tuesday, April 11th, 8am

The video that Malcolm posted was played into the basement where the six prisoners lay trapped on their gurneys. Through the night there had been tears, tantrums, and individuals trying to scream out. The gags held firm. After the video played, Malcolm opened the door and carried in a tray with more bottles of water on it. Alongside them were six Kellogg's breakfast bars.

"Morning everyone," he said with an upbeat, chirpy tone, "you'll have had a tough night I expect, not much sleeping going on. Last night was quite horrendous, wasn't it? Well, today will be quite boring for you all, once I've given you all a drink and something to eat, sorry it's only breakfast bars I'm afraid, I will leave you until after 9 tonight." He continued talking as he approached Chris on the bed. "The TV will go on just before 9 though so you can watch how it all pans out on the chair." He removed Chris' gag.

"I need the toilet," spluttered Chris.

"Oh no, I forgot to mention, you'll not be getting up, I am sorry." He raised the straw, "You see there is six of you, some of you will die, some of you won't," gesturing with his left hand, then the right as he flipped between the two possible outcomes "but I don't have time to give each one of you bathroom breaks. Besides, don't you watch the movies? Allowing you time to get up increases the risk of you trying to escape. So, no, you'll need to just do your business there, and if you leave here alive I'm sure you can just grab a quick shower." He unwrapped the Kellogg's bar and Gregory took a bite. "And anyway," sniffing the air, "I think tough guy Gregory over there already gave up on the idea of a bathroom break." He finished with Chris and replaced his gag. Over the next fifteen minutes, he completed the rounds in the room. The others didn't say too much, some refusing to eat, some taking just a drink. Once finished he gathered up all the wrappers and placed them on the tray along with the bottles, balancing them in one hand as he headed to the door, turning before he left the room. "Get some rest, I'll see you all later." With that Malcolm closed the door and ascended the stairs.

Tuesday, April 11th, 10.30am

"I've just left Russ's home boss, we'll have round the clock presence front and back of the property. He refused to come with us." Burnham's update did not interest Ford who glanced at the clock, 10.30am, then back down at the TV. The news was showing highlights of MacHray's morning press conference. It had not gone well, the questions being asked were horrendous, anything from "Should George have shot himself?" to "Are the police underfunded?" This was a turning into a political nightmare for MacHray and those she answered to.

"Are they all here?" Asked Ford.

"Yes, boss, all in the breakout room, waiting for you. They are scared shitless now." Burnham continued, "So, Chilton is on profiling, what do you want me on?"

"Malcolm. I want properties, previous addresses hangouts. Let Chilton work on the gays and matching everything up with them and his theory." He looked over at the board, "We need to know where he is, where he could be, knock every door down if you have to. He must be living local enough, and holding them local, Wendy's body was dumped not long after, so he can't be far." He stood up and began walking out of the room. "I'm going to be a fox in a hen house."

As he entered the visitor's room, the chattering that was happening between them all ceased immediately. He looked at the clock on the wall, 11am. "Ten hours," he thought, "ten hours to save a life." He scanned the room, they were all here, all six of them.

He looked at Mrs. Johnston, a familiar face looked back at him. "Why do I know your face?" This mother looked back at him as he asked, her eyes scanning him, trying to recall where she knew his face from. Before she could answer, the penny dropped in Ford's memory. "High School … you went to St Columbus High?" He asked.

"Jimboy?" The woman had been close to tears, but she now remembered this man clearly. "Yes, it's me, Nicky." She instantly hugged Jim, held him close for a couple of seconds, he gently returned the hug but didn't want to get too close.

Releasing the hug, Jim stood back from her. "I hope we have plenty of time to catch up Nicky, but I have some serious work to do. Your son," he turned to the rest of the room, "all of your relatives, are in serious danger and I need to find them." He looked back at Nicky, "tell me about your son."

"He doesn't deserve this," she whimpered, "I don't deserve this we've been through enough, he was a child that made a mistake." She looked at Jim, "Please Jim, you have to find him."

Ford was forcing his will to stay professional. As he spoke he recalled memories of Nicky as a teenager, they had been close for a while, living as typical teenagers, weekend drinking and getting up to mischief. As he considered how strange the wheels of fate worked, bringing them back together after what must have been twenty years, he turned to address everyone, remaining professional. "So what do we have? We know that Malcolm worked in a Social Services office as a cleaner, most of you have had some dealings in the same office." He turned to Mr. Ritchie, "I don't believe we've met, sir." Mr. Ritchie stood up and offered a hand that was accepted.

"Roy Ritchie, the son of a bitch has my girl, Claire." He was clearly a proud man, stood upright, "What can I do to help?"

"Well, Mr. Ritchie, you and your daughter, you are my enigma." Ford walked to a chair in the corner and sat down, "From everything I have found out there is no scandal about you two. I can't find anything, so unless you are very good at hiding it, I remain confused. Everyone else has a skeleton in the closet that I believe this man Malcolm intends to expose, but not you."

"Now wait a dam minute," interrupted Michael Wenham. "Myself and my partner are decent people too, I've never been down to Social Services for anything in my life, and neither has David."

Ford, swivelled in his chair to face Michael, "Michael Wenham I presume," Ford did not offer this man a hand to shake.

"Yes, and I don't like you lumping David and I in with everyone else," he was an uptight sod, Ford's distaste for him was instant.

"Well, that's a very good point Mr. Wenham, you are not on file at Social Services so Malcolm could not have targeted you because of something you've been questioned about." Ford leaned forward a little, staring straight into Michael's eye, "So what does he have on you?"

"What?!" Michael was mortified, "How fucking dare you, David and I are good, decent people. There is nothing, we raise money for charity for fuck sake." As he said this Michael stood up, "I don't have to sit here and listen to this! If this is what you call police work, I'm appalled. "

"Sit down Mr. Wenham, I'm not done yet." Ford remained seated, leaning forward, and just glanced up at Michael. Michael showed defiance for a second, then thought better of it.

"Am I under arrest?" asked Michael.

"Don't be stupid, but if I don't catch this guy either you or David will be dead on Sunday night, so I suggest you co-operate and tell me what I need to know to help solve this puzzle. And tell me quick because that woman there is next," he gestured a nod to Nicola, who still had tears in her eyes, "so, what's your skeleton?"

"What the fuck, so I have one but this old guy here doesn't?" Michael pointed at Roy. Roy didn't flinch, just folded his arms with contempt of the man pointing the finger.

"Yup, that's the way I see it," Ford was keeping his gaze on Michael, looking for the eye twitch, that little bead of sweat, the tapping foot, picking of nails, that tell-tale sign that his prey was nervous. "You see Mr. Wenham, five more people may have to walk to that chair before you, and if you are holding something back that could prevent that from happening you need to start talking." The rest of the group seemed to pay a little more attention after he had said that. "Tell me about the Samuel Higgins Trust?" With the mention of that, Michael shifted in his seat, in an involuntary motion which Ford noticed, the trigger that confirmed in Ford's mind that this man was dirty. People can lie but very few people are good liars, and this man Michael was not as good as he thought he needed to be.

"What about it?" Michael's voice stayed constant, he had that part of the act perfected. "David and I raise money for children suffering from cancer, we fund special days for them, give them some happiness until a cure can be found."

"Nice Bentley in my parking lot, Mr. Wenham," Ford watched his face, a frown line appeared on Michael's forehead. He turned from

Michael immediately, not giving him time to respond. "Harry?" The Asian man in the corner turned his head towards Ford.

"Yes," he was lethargic, seemingly uncaring about his predicament, "Your father is not a well man?"

"He forgets things, I look after him, you already know all that I am sure," Harry looked back out the window, "and I know I have to make a choice tomorrow, I've pretty much already made up my mind." The room turned to look at him, "he's old, he's lived his life, plus he can't remember shit anyway, it would be a blessing for him."

"You fucker," Roy barked, "That man raised your skinny ass, and you're going to let him die!"

"Roy, calm please," Ford gestured a hand, palm down to the ground, "Harry, here's the thing. I cannot tell you what to do, no way, but we now have armed police outside Mr. Russ' house after the video that was posted this morning. The public aren't happy, check out the forums, the media, they're gunning for Mr. Russ, and his life is not going to be a quiet one for a while." Harry didn't look away from the window he was pretending to look out of. Ford, looked toward Martin, as he caught his eye, Martin looked toward the ground. "Martin Imbeault ... sorry, I hope I pronounced that right ... you have a string of allegations against you. Nothing upheld, but I am wondering what this Malcolm might have on you that he's so upset about?" Martin didn't look up from the floor, didn't answer, he just kept staring. Ford sensed it wasn't the time to press him, maybe not in front of the whole group, besides they were still only allegations, he didn't want to cross a line, not yet.

Claire Papadopoulos sat crying in the corner. Ford noticed that she'd had time to do her make-up and hair this morning, before coming to the station. "You're having an affair, Claire," she looked at Ford as he mentioned her name, "it's ok, it's not uncommon. I just don't quite know how Malcolm could know you. You aren't known to Social Services that I am aware of?"

"No," she pulled a tissue from a box on the table and dabbed her eyes, "I think it's from last year. I recognise the man in the picture on the news, I didn't want to say anything before, but I don't want anyone to die." She burst into sobs again. Nicola got to her feet and moved to the chair next to her, placing a consoling arm over her back and reaching for more tissues. Despite her own emotional state, she was a caring person. Seeing another woman cry and being able to console her gave her something to distract her momentarily.

"Anything you can tell me, Claire," Ford asked gently.

"Well, there was this guy, last year in the bar. He was cute, muscular, and he bought me a drink. Next thing I know I'm in the bathroom with him ..." she paused and looked up, everyone was now looking at her, "well that was it initially, but the guy was in the bar the next week, but I was with Greg then, he tried to buy me another drink, but I told him to fuck off cos my boyfriend was there. That was the last I saw of him, but I'm sure it's that guy, Malcolm." She continued sobbing.

"What pub were you in?" Ford reached for his notepad.

"The Dog and Duck, in Harringay."

"Well that's something new, thank you, Claire," with that Ford stood up. "I want you all to stay at the station if possible, I'll get something sorted for you to sleep somewhere. Speak to your families but it will help us if you are close by." He glanced at the clock, 11.25, and left the room reaching for his phone. "Burnham, I need you to get to the Dog and Duck in Harringay, Claire Papadopoulos only went and shagged Malcolm in the men's room about a year ago, that's the connection between the two of them. Maybe the landlord or one of the locals knows something." He poured another coffee on his way to the Ops Room. "Chilton, tell me something I don't know." Ford had a new bounce in his voice, he was happy they were chipping away at the evidence.

"Well boss, Wenham, and Sutherland are definitely dirty, but to be honest, proving it will need a warrant and team of financial lawyers, and we just don't have the time." Chilton closed a file with their pictures on the front.

"You can stop your trace on the bombshell, she's confessed to having bathroom sex with Malcolm about a year ago, I have Brad heading down to the pub where it happened in Harringay, you never know someone might say something." Ford pulled up a seat in front of the board which was having information added to it all the time. "What about Malcolm, anything knew?"

"Well we are searching previous known addresses all relatively local in this area of London, he has a lot, to be honest, but most have been rentals, all with new tenants in them. I have men going door to door around those properties anyway. As for his past," Chilton picked up Ford's coffee and walked to the board, "oh, thanks boss," he smirked, and Ford raised an eyebrow. "Well, both parents passed away in his late teens, and his sister committed suicide when she was just thirteen, he was only fifteen. He stayed with an aunty until she passed away when he was twenty-two, all seems clean after that. After that he has a couple of jobs that we know of, then ten years at Sireon, all minimum wage, all monkey work. No previous convictions." He turned to Ford. That was all he had.

Ford let out a sigh, a deep long groan followed, incited by a lack of sleep and nature of the case. "Fuck, fuck, fuck," he said softly, "ok, so we know who he is, we think we know why he is doing it, that he certainly has the balls to follow his plan through, we just don't know where he is." He looked up at the board, pausing for a second. "What do we know about the sister's suicide?"

"I'm still trying to find out details," Chilton replied, "rough neighbourhood, poor upbringing, in and out of care. It looks like it was a pretty open and shut case of a girl jumping off a tower block." Ford froze, his memory stirred but he kept his focus on the board.

"Anything on the van?" asked Ford.

"No, nothing." replied Chilton, "With no plates, it's a difficult thing to find. No reports of stolen vans of that make and model in the area."

"Ok, let's see what Brad gets from the pub. I know Nicky Johnston," he said looking at Chilton.

Raising an eyebrow, "Really?" Ash was curious.

"We went to high school together," Ford stood up and took his now empty mug back from the younger detective, "Strange way to meet someone from your past, isn't it? Keep me posted on the previous addresses."

August, 2010

"Enjoy your coffee," he told her. Matt had just returned from a week-long work trip, leaving his wife to look after his two stepsons. She looked exhausted and just needed to get out of the house, he was also tired and was happy for her to head off as he spied the couch and figured a nap wouldn't do him any harm.

"What about Chris?" She asked, looking towards the staircase.

He sighed, "You need a break Hun, leave him, he'll have to cope and get used to the fact that he can't be tied to your hip."

"Are you sure?" She was nervous. Her son Chris had never liked her going out, and it wasn't anything to do with Matt, he'd been part of his life since he was at nursery, but still he was a needy child even at thirteen.

"Listen, go and have your coffee, say hi to your sister and chill, I'll take a nap and if he kicks off he can stay in his room," Matt sat down on the couch, "it's not like there is much more he can break up there anyway." Nicola winced at this, she knew Chris was a difficult child, but she hated that her husband reminded her of the damage he caused to his room when he went off on one of his rages.

"Ok," she sighed, "Call me if you have any bother." She walked to the hall and picked up her car keys.

"Mum!!" Chris came bolting down the stairs shouting, "Mum, where are you going!" The young teenager threw himself around his mother's waist.

"Your Mum's popping out, Chris, don't cause a scene," Matt sat bolt upright from his reclined position, he looked at Nicola with a stern face, his eyes begging her not to give in. Chris buried his face into her body and began stamping his feet.

"Matt, you won't get any rest if he stays here," she looked guilty when she spoke, "I'll take him this time." Matt stayed silent, there was no point in arguing anymore, they had danced this tango far too many times, he should have known Chris was listening and he would be down. He was annoyed that she gave into him so often, he genuinely wanted her to have peace and quiet, but then he also didn't want to sit and listen to the kid smashing up his room again.

"Fine," Matt reclined and closed his eyes, "see you later." Nicola stood there upset. She couldn't keep both of them happy, a frustration she had lived with for years.

"James is at his Dads," she offered, "I'll see you in a couple of hours." Matt's silence hurt as much as Chris' dependence on her, she took a final glance at him sitting with his eyes closed, before heading out of the door.

The drive to her sister's house was quiet. She never wanted to challenge Chris about his behaviour when they were alone, he had this ability to make her feel incredibly guilty about the split from his biological Dad even though it was him that was unfaithful. He also hated Matt, this guy that he felt monopolised her time and told him what he could and couldn't do. She knew this but said nothing.

She opened the back door and walked in through the kitchen, Chris remained in the garden where his young cousin Kelly-Ann was playing on the swing.

"You got Chris again," asked Katrina, the younger of the two sisters. She did not sound surprised, every visit her sister made for a coffee, her nephew was there on her tail.

"Please don't," Nicola asked as she slumped on the sofa, "just get that kettle on will ya." The door from the hallway opened as her brother in law walked in, "Hey bro, Matt's just back if you want a beer tonight."

"Back from his skive is he?" Keith was a big lump of a lad, a manual worker compared to the paperwork Matt shuffled around, best friends, but very different people. "Tell him I'll be down The Oak about 8 and he's on the tab." He leaned over and gave Nicola a quick peck on the cheek.

"Kelly-Ann get in here now," Katrina yelled from the kitchen that looked out onto the garden. Her voice seemed alarmed.

"Sis?" Nicola got up from her seat as Katrina opened the back door and ushered in her daughter. She was crying as Keith scooped her up in his arms, looking at his wife who had gone chalk white.

"What is it?" he asked.

His wife looked at her sister, "You've got to go!" Her words were sharp and blunt. Nicola looked at her and saw a face she had never seen.

"Ok," she uttered stepping to the back door, "Chris, we're going." She grabbed her handbag and walked down the side alley back to her car with Chris close behind. Climbing into the driver's seat she waited until her son had clicked his seatbelt. "What happened?" She asked, Chris just shrugged his shoulders and said nothing.

As she arrived at her own home she was still confused. Her sister had never spoken to her like that before and she was worried. Opening the front door Matt sat bolt upright looking at his watch, he had been enjoying a nap on his couch, expecting his wife to be at least a couple of hours.

"Was she not in?" he enquired, stretching his arms out wide after his twenty winks.

"Aye, she was, but she's in a properly weird mood." She sat down on the couch next to him as Chris sat on the other one. Matt cast his gaze over to the other couch, his instincts told him something was wrong. "She was putting the kettle on and then suddenly said I had to leave." His wife clearly looked rattled and a little upset.

At that moment Matt's phone rang, he pulled it out his pocket "It's Keith, hold on," he answered the phone as he walked into the hallway. "Mate what's up?"

"I'm driving round to the shop, I need to speak to you now," Keith's words and tone were not welcoming.

"Mate, whatever it is just come round, I'll crack a beer," Matt remained upbeat, despite sensing something was very wrong.

"Round the shop now." With that, Keith hung up.

Matt looked at the phone, and then back into the living room, "Keith wants me to meet him round the shop?" Nicola stared at him and noticed his eyes flip across to Chris sat on the other couch. "I'll be right back." With that, he slipped his shoes on and headed out the door. The shop was literally a hundred yards around the corner, a thirty-second walk, but in that thirty seconds, every conceivable scenario was racing through his mind. He had known Keith for years, he had even introduced him and Katrina, he knew his moods, he knew his banter, but this was something different. As he rounded the corner he saw the silver Mercedes pulling up, he rounded the front of the car and climbed in the passenger door.

He stared at Keith for a second, Keith's gaze was directed towards Matt's house, even though it was not quite in view. "Keith?" Matt spoke first.

"If I go in that house I'm going to kill him," Keith did not move his gaze.

"What the fuck is going on mate, you're scaring me," Matt knew Keith was a big guy, but he had never shown this kind of aggression.

"He's been fiddling with Kelly-Ann." Silence filled the air after that statement. Matt sat stunned, his heart felt like it stopped. He was panicking at what he had just heard come out of his best friend's mouth. Keith's body made a reaching movement as he flung open the driver's door and vomited into the gutter. Matt knew, he knew immediately Keith was speaking the truth, but he felt obligated to at least attempt to defend him. It was almost like everything about that little boy made suddenly made sense.

"Mate, come on ..." his voiced wobbled.

"Katrina saw his big fat hand in her knickers in the garden," Keith turned his stare to Matt for the first time, "I'm going home to phone the police. I just wanted to tell you that."

Matt stared, his voice tried to come out of his mouth several times, the beginning of his next sentence got started and stopped in his head over and over again, and when something finally came out it trembled. "You're telling me I need to go home and tell my wife her son is a pervert?" Matt stared at him, his eyes were begging for Keith to tell him it was a sick joke. He sat for what felt like an eternity, Keith just stared directly ahead of him. Matt's hand was shaking as he reached for the door handle and pulled on it, stepping out onto the street. He had barely closed it as Keith accelerated away.

He stood in the middle of the street, not taking anything in except the last two minutes in that car. Only when an oncoming car blared his horn at him did he finally he step onto the path, his legs heavy with dread. He walked towards his house, up the front stairs, opening the door and stepping into the hallway. Walking into the living room, he glanced at his wife, knowing he was about to destroy her world, and then his face turned into spite as he looked towards Chris.

"Matt, what is it?" she asked.

Tuesday, April 11th, 12.30pm

Malcolm sat in the front room of the house above the basement. With a plate on his lap, he kept the news on as he bit into his bacon sandwich. He was finding it amusing that a "specialist psychologist" was providing an explanation into the survival instinct of the human being and why Mr. Russ had not pulled the trigger. "He was a fucking coward," Malcolm said out loud.

He looked around at the living room. He liked what the Alderman's had done to the place since they moved in. The couch was cream, the room bland and basic, but it worked. "I like your living room," he called through to the next room.

At that moment there was a knock at the door. Malcolm froze. It could be nothing, a delivery driver, a gas man here to check the meter. There was another knock at the door, then the noise of the letterbox being pushed open "Hello, it's the police, could we have a quick word?" The letterbox snapped back shut. Malcolm could hear voices on the front step. For a minute they continued, the feint squeak of a police radio, then movement back down the stairs. For at least ten minutes Malcolm sat in his chair, he finished his sandwich and gave it enough time to be comfortable that the officers had given up and left.

Getting up from the couch, he moved through to the open plan dining room. He glanced to his left "Thanks for the sandwich," he said to the seven dead bodies wrapped in plastic in the corner. He moved through to the kitchen and placed the plate in the sink, glancing out of the back window at his van parked on the rear-drive. "We may have to move house then."

The Police had left the front door, moving on to the houses up the road. Malcolm returned to the living room and peeked out of the bay window, he was confident they were just going door to door but even so, he knew he would not be able to spend the week in this house. The basement had been perfect but staying too long in one place was risky which he had known would always be the case. He would wait until tonight's events and then move his prisoners.

Tuesday, April 11th, 4pm

"Malcolm has been described as a bit of a loaner by the pub landlord, but nothing sinister. He said he'd phoned the hotline about Malcolm drinking in his pub, it must be still filtering through to us." Burnham was relaying from his notepad to Ford and Chilton. This was the first time they had all been together since they were at Trafalgar.   "He said he's been a local for years, popped in occasionally enough to have his face known, but not his name. Didn't really keep any company, and this was confirmed by a couple of bar dogs that were already in for their liquid lunch."

"What about the previous properties," Ford addressed Burnham again. "Well, we've been to twelve properties, pretty much all different letting agents, eight tenants at home, I'll have officers go back to the others around tea time, people should be home from work. They are all described as "not first-class properties" by the door to door teams. We also have door to door checks going on around the pub and some of the most recent properties that he has lived at. It's arduous but might turn up something."

"Well, Malcolm is no rich guy, so that suits." Ford pushed a packet of donuts to the centre of the table, "take them away, I've got a figure to look after."

"Aye right boss," chortled Ash, "the figure you're looking after is MacHray's." Ash had stopped his mouth from talking too late. "Sorry boss, out of line."

"It's alright," Ford said, getting to his feet, he walked to the board, "she does have a tight rack." He smirked with his back to his team. Chilton and Burnham looked at each other and smiled, it was a good feeling to work with Ford, he was a hard ass but could have a laugh with the boys too. Ford glanced up at the clock. 4pm. "Fuck," he said out loud but quietly. "This guy is a fucking whacko and he is hidden in plain sight. He isn't shy, he knows we know who he is, his face is all over the media, and yet he is holed up somewhere with six people and no one knows where that is."

Ford turned to his team. "What do you think Mrs. Johnstone is going to do," asked Chilton. He was just saying what the three of them were thinking. If they didn't catch a lucky break it would be 9pm eventually.

"I think we'll be cleaning up Trafalgar Square." Ford had no doubt with her. With everything that lad had put her through, she had protected him the whole time, and her son came first because she truly believed he could be a good boy.

Tuesday, April 11th, 6pm

Ford led Nicola into an empty room. He offered a cup of water, "Please take a seat." He gestured to the chair by the desk as he sat in the other one. "It's 6pm, I wanted to know if you needed anything or you need to speak to anyone?"

"There's no one left to," she uttered. Glancing around the room she then looked back at Ford. "There's a good boy in there somewhere, Jim, I know he can have a good life. What he did ... what he did we all tried to keep quiet for my niece's sake, but it was me who went to the police in the first place. They took him from me because my brother was threatening him, when I got him back he'd gotten worse. He sat in his room all the time, he became insular and angry at everyone. I think he knows what he did was very wrong, and he knows the damage it's caused. But he was just a child himself and maybe I'm to blame, I don't know, it's a really messed up situation. It all happened six years ago." She glanced down at the floor. "I feel so sorry for my brother and little Kelly-Ann, I cry a lot about it. No one comes round anymore, no one visits. Except the social services once a fortnight, always once a fortnight and they say the same old thing. You see, he's nineteen now, I know he'd never do anything like that again, but he's lonely too. He doesn't see his cousins, my family, and his Dad is not in his life, his younger brother hates him, my husband left, I'm all he's got."

She reached into her purse and pulled out a folded piece of paper. She offered it to Jim, "One of your policewomen found me some paper, but she couldn't find me an envelope. Could you put this in it and give it to Chris for me. He'll be so alone but I want him to know he has a future."

Jim's heart sank as he knew she'd made her decision. He took the paper from Nicola, kept it gently in his hand and placed his other hand on her shoulder. "I'm still trying to find this man, Nicky," he said quietly.

She looked up at Jim with the tiniest of smiles, "I know you are, thank you. But I'm ready for what I need to do." The two of them stared at each other for a moment, Jim fought back the urge to pull her into his arms and hold her tight. "Can I tell you something, Jim?" She never looked up, but Ford sensed he did not need to give her permission. "In the weeks after Katrina saw him do what he did, it was chaotic. There was so much going on and all I tried to do was understand. I had convinced myself it was just once, that my little boy had made an innocent mistake. Then one evening he was calm, he was sitting on his mattress on the floor in his room, and I was sitting next to him." She paused, about to tell Ford something she had not spoken out about in six years, something she had only shared with the social workers. "I asked him how many times, I was listening to what everyone else was saying about him, and I wanted them all to be liars. I wanted to know that they were exaggerating. And then he told me." She was shaking as Ford held her hand. "Six months he told me." Sobbing through she continued. "Then I asked him what he did, what he actually did to my poor niece, and what he told me I will never forget." She stopped talking, she had shared her secret.

The silence was broken with a knock at the door.

"Come in," Jim called.

Burnham and Chilton entered, they looked concerned. "Boss, he's posted another video. Mrs. Johnston, you'll want to watch this, it was loaded about twenty minutes ago." He placed the iPad he was holding on the desk and pressed play.

Malcolm's voice made him sound like he was telling a story.

"Good afternoon Britain. Last night you witnessed a wife-beating coward allow his wife to be murdered. This evening Nicola Johnstone will hopefully sit in my chair, but let me tell you about her dilemma, her son Chris is a troubled youth. You see, when Chris was 13 he targeted his 7-year-old cousin, abused her in her bedroom while their parents drank coffee downstairs. He raped her. He was never charged, and from what I can tell about his behaviour since then has never felt remorse. His mother protects him as any mother should, but her life is now one of loneliness, isolated from her family because she looks after her delinquent son. This is a child that could grow up to repeat his actions. I do hope you all tune in to see what Mrs. Johnstone does at 9pm."

The video ended. Nicola broke down in tears, "noooooo, everyone knows, everyone knows now, he'll never be able to live." She looked at the three men, tears streaming down her face, "it's not fair, he won't do it again. I know he won't." She threw herself at Jim, collapsing onto his chest and he instinctively drew her in with his big arms, comforting his old friend. As she sobbed he looked at his two colleagues, he was angry but not with them, he was angry with Malcolm.

After a few minutes, the three men left the room. "It's coming up for 7," said Chilton, "we need to find that van. I'm going to say something, and you guys might not like it." The other two men stopped in the corridor and looked at him, "just after 9," he continued, "a white Mercedes Box van will be driving around a certain area. He's either going to dump a body," he cast his eyes back at the room they had just left, "or release her son. We need to have these streets mobbed with patrol cars, you never know we might get lucky."

"I'll make it happen," said Ford reaching for his phone, "Brad, can you make sure someone is with her, make sure she gets food if she needs it. I'll come back in an hour." Addressing Chilton, "I want you down at Trafalgar Square, that video is going to stir up the heathens looking for a paedophile to lynch, it's going to get ugly." With that Ford walked away dialing MacHray on his mobile.

"Alison, did you see it?" He said.

"Yes," she replied, "he really wants the nation to get behind him, he's talking like it's a crusade he is on. Christ, Jim, we're going to get to 9 o'clock again without finding him aren't we?"

He winced, "Yes Ma'am," it was the truth. That lucky lead he had been praying for had not turned up yet. "I'll take her down to the square, we know why they are here, we know he is trying to make them pay for their mistakes in life, but we don't know where he is. I need as many squads out as possible tonight please, we're looking for the van around 9pm, anything that might be out of the ordinary." He paused, and then added, "And I need a private ambulance at the Square."

"You think she's going to go through with it?" MacHray asked bluntly.

"I have no doubt."

Tuesday, April 11th 8.45pm

The convoy of cars drove towards Trafalgar Square for the second time that week. This time Ford sat in the back with Nicola, Burnham was in the front with Chilton driving. She sat with wet eyes, but still and very calm. There was no conversation in the car and soon they pulled up. The noise of the crowd could be heard from inside the car. The only people close were the police, the cordon had given them plenty of space. He looked at his watch.

"It's 8.45 Nicola, I say we give it a few minutes before we get out." Nicola sat there staring straight ahead. Jim glanced out the back window. About twenty yards away was parked a black private ambulance. "Fuckers could at least keep it out of sight," he thought.

Eventually, Jim climbed out of the car, Burnham followed. Walking around to the other side of the car, Jim placed his hand on the handle and took a deep breath. He opened the door and leaned in, "You don't have to do this."

She looked up at him, drew a tissue from her handbag, dried her eyes, replaced the handbag on the seat and climbed out of the car. She cast her gaze around the crowd surrounding most of the square. Bright lights shone down from cranes up above, cameras over to the right. "I want to speak to them please, Jim." She asked, "do you think that would be ok?"

Ford looked at Burnham, and then back at her again. "I can't see that it would hurt, we've got twelve minutes."

She walked towards the cameras, journalists interrupted their reports, many on live feeds. As she approached they became quiet, holding out their microphones. Ford and Burnham were either side of her. "My name is Nicola Johnstone," she began, "you've all heard what Malcolm has to say about my son, and I am sure you have all formed your opinions. I am a good mother, I have tried very hard to bring up my son well, with morals. He made a mistake, a grave one that I cannot undo. He hates himself for it and will always hate himself, that's why he is so angry. Please don't persecute him when I am gone." With that she turned and walked away, heading towards the chair. The journalists said nothing stunned in silence. Ford walked after her, about halfway between her and the chair he stopped her, and she turned.

He looked into her eyes, she seemed peaceful. "I'm so sorry," he said quietly.

She put her arm on his shoulder. "You didn't do this," She replied. Her eyes were warm, telling Jim she really was ok, she placed her hand on his and patted it. She then allowed her hand to fall from his shoulder and turned and walked towards the chair, Ford stood still.

As she approached the chair from the side, she saw the gun for the first time. She reached down and picked it up, she looked at it for a second, and then took a seat. Her movement was smooth, no nerves filled her body, she was calm and sure of herself.

Ford looked on, he was terrified. She was a good woman. As the first chime of Big Ben rang out, she smoothly raised her arm, opened her mouth and pulled the trigger. The crack of the gun echoed around the square, screams filled the air from the crowd and Nicola's head snapped straight back, and her body slumped sideways off the chair, with the gun hitting the ground. Ford was up to full speed before the second chime, and he knelt down beside her, his fingers reached for her pulse on her throat, a useless gesture. He placed his hand on her forehead and wept. As Burnham and Chilton joined his side, he looked up at them. "This has to fucking stop."

Tuesday, 11th April, 9.10pm

As the door to the cellar opened there were moans throughout the room. They had been allowed to watch Mrs. Johnstone place the gun in her mouth and save her son. Malcolm, wearing a face mask, walked over to the gurney where Chris lay, he placed a rag over Chris' nose and mouth and held it there for a couple of minutes. As he held it there he cast his eyes around the other five, beneath his mask he was smiling, and that smile showed in his eyes. Chris' eyes closed.

Unfastening the straps, and unlocking the handcuffs, he lifted Chris onto his shoulder, walked out the door and up the stairs. At the top of the stairs was the hallway, Malcolm crossed it and entered the dining room, placing Chris on the dining room table onto a length of plastic he had rolled out earlier. He removed his facemask and returned down the stairs to close and lock the door.

Folding in the edges of the plastic, he then reached for the ends of the bungee cords he had laid beneath and fastened them around Chris's body. He hoisted the unconscious lump onto his shoulder again, and moved towards the back door, ducking as he moved through the various doorways. Pulling down on the handle, the door opened outwards, he glanced at the neighbouring properties. The high fences and the climbing plants offered quite a bit of seclusion, but he needed to be careful all the same. Assessing that the coast was clear, he walked up the garden path to the van at the end, the rear roller door already open halfway. He dropped Chris into the back of the lorry and quietly pulled the door down, lifting over one of the catches.

He walked to the back door, lifted the handle and locked it with his keys. Pulling up the hood of his jersey he shuffled up the side of the van, there wasn't much room between that and the garden wall. Climbing into the cab, he started the engine, and pulled away slowly, keeping the revs to a minimum. The back drive lead out onto a dirt alley between the rows of houses. He turned right off the driveway and headed down the lane. After a hundred yards the lane was intersected by a side street, before carrying on between the next row of houses. This continued for four more streets, with Malcolm driving very slowly. He turned left after the fourth street and navigated various back roads. He never made it to a main road during his drive, and ten minutes later pulled up towards the end of a street. He looked around, he was parked next to the side of a house, no others looked directly onto him. He jumped out of the cab, moved to the back of the vehicle and hoisted up the roller door. Grabbing Chris' body, he cradled his legs and neck, lifting him to the path. He carefully placed him down, pulled down the roller door and returned to the cab. The street was wide enough to perform a three-point turn, and he traced his route back the way he came. On his return journey, he noticed an elderly man with a peak cap walking his dog. The man glanced at him but didn't seem to pay much attention, it didn't matter too much, he was moving his prisoners tonight.

Tuesday, April 11th, 9.15pm

As Ford returned to the car, Burnham opened the door for him. In the crowd, there were screams, chants, and angry people shouting obscenities. Ford was in a state of tunnel vision, blocking out everything. He glanced over at Nicola's body. Medics had covered her with a blanket and were preparing a body bag. Officers darted here and there, scurrying around doing what they were supposed to be doing. Burnham was talking to him, telling him to get in the car. He bowed his head and climbed onto the back seat, Chilton was climbing in behind the wheel, and Burnham took the passenger seat. As the car pulled away Ford glanced down at the handbag in the seat. He stared at it for ages. Then he looked at his hands, they had specks of her blood on them, as did his trousers and his shirt. There wasn't much talking on the ride back to the Yard. Ford fumbled in the jacket pocket he had put Nicola's letter to her son in, and pulled it out. He held onto to it tightly, his head swimming with a thousand thoughts a second as they crossed through London, street lamps flickering over the letter and the handbag.

"When we find her son take him straight to General. He'll need a full check-up." He sat back up in his seat as they pulled into the

Yard. He was coming to himself. He was forcing it and he needed to as he knew he had work to do. "I need a stiff one, boys, come on."

They walked into his office, Jim sat behind his desk, Ash and Brad sat in the two chairs opposite. He slid the large desk drawer open and lifted out a bottle of Famous Grouse. He unscrewed the cap and grabbed three mugs from the drawer as well. He poured three large measures, his colleagues lifted their mugs. "To Nicola," said Jim. With that the door opened, MacHray walked in and leant on the unit along the side of the wall. Brad made a movement to offer her a seat and she patted his shoulder, instructing him to stay where he was.

"I'll have one of those though, Jim." She gestured to the whiskey. He reached back into the drawer and pulled out a plastic cup.

"It's all I got, Alison." He poured her a measure, she lifted it and gestured to the toast Jim had made. "This is fucked up situation guys, we need to find him. I want patrols going garden to garden in each house within the target area. Anything that looks out of place I want reported." He paused.

Alison stood up, downed her whiskey. "All three of you are doing everything you need to be doing. I would never say this outside this room, but sometimes whackos can hide in plain sight. This Malcolm has a plan, a plan he has clearly been working on for years, and when an insane man believes he is sane, and he has planned something for so long, there is little you can do to stop him." She walked towards the door. As she turned back, "You three, get some sleep. When the lad turns up I'll get someone to look after him, I want you fresh for tomorrow. Go home, get some sleep, a shower and shave, come back first thing and crack this." She walked out the door, looking back briefly "and that's a direct order, Jim."

As her heels walked off down the corridor Jim looked at his team. "Right, she makes perfect sense. We've been at this for nearly two straight days." He stood up, knocking back his whiskey and returning the bottle to the drawer. "We've learned a lot in two days, tomorrow we'll catch him. Keep your phones on just in case." With that, the three men left the office.

Driving home the image of Nicola pulling the trigger just fifteen feet from him kept going through his mind, over and over, taunting him. His brain started processing bizarre "what if" scenarios, the whizz of thoughts hurt his head. He pulled over abruptly, fired open the car door and threw up on the road. Slowly pulling his head back upright, he closed the door and returned to the road.

As he entered his dark house, his feet kicked some mail from the mat, he walked immediately upstairs without touching a light switch. On the top landing, he kicked off his shoes one by one, loosened his tie as he walked into his bedroom, removed his phone and placed it on the cabinet, and finally collapsed on the bed.

He woke as his phone was giving short little bursts of vibration on the cabinet. He sat up, still in clothes, grabbed his phone and with his other hand wiped his eyes with a squeezing motion, noticing the bloodstains still on them as he did. The time said 6.30am. It was a text from Alison:

CHRIS JOHNSTONE SAFE AND WELL. FOUND ON A SIDE STREET. IN THE ROYAL GENERAL WITH MEN POSTED. SEE YOU WHEN YOU COME IN.

That was good news. It meant Malcolm was playing fair. He headed to the ensuite and took a shower. Digging out a clean suit after shaving he got dresses, then headed to the kitchen before he ran a capsule into the coffee machine. While it was brewing he text Brad and Ash in a group message:

BOY IS SAFE, BRAD GET TO THE HOSPITAL AND SPEAK WITH THE BOY SEE WHAT HE CAN TELL YOU. ASH MEET ME IN THE OPS ROOM AT 7.30.

Within moments Brad replied saying he was on his way, Ash said he was already there. "Good lad," thought Jim. He grabbed his keys and headed in.

Wednesday, April 12th 7.30am

Jim put the incoming call on the loudspeaker in the car. "Ash, what is it?"

"Boss, we got a call, we know where he is," Chilton sounded like he was running. "I've called for an armed response unit and we're assembling now."

"How? What? Tell me where, I'll meet you there," Ford barked with a grin.

"Harringay, 21 Duke Street. I got a call from the hotline team. A local letting agents got a call during the night from a neighbour of one of their properties, about a white panel van going to and from the property during the night. Apparently, the woman thought someone was doing a moonlight flit. The letting agent thought she should call it in."

"For fuck sake, that's got to be him. I'm heading there now." Ford put his foot down, it was a half-hour drive even going at speed.

As he drove into the street blue tape was lifted to let him closer to the property. They had already entered, and he could see armed police were walking back down the front steps. As he pulled to a halt he could see one man spewing his guts next to a squad car. He jumped out of the car and glanced up at the steps. He saw Chilton at the top of them. His initial thoughts were that they were all dead, all of them. He ran over, hustled past a couple of men coming down the stairs and stared at Chilton. "What?" He barked.

"They're not here boss," the younger detective said, his voice was shaking, his face white "but it's been a massacre for someone else." Ford looked confused and he darted past Chilton. As he walked into the property he could smell something musty. He passed a living room on his left, stairs down the way on his right, but there were men in the room ahead. As he walked in his eyes widened, he held onto the door. In the corner were what appeared to be seven corpses. A large body at the bottom, and then gradually getting smaller, stacked in a pile. They were all wrapped individually in plastic, blood-smeared the inside. Looking at the corpses it was evident that the top few were that of young children, and not the prisoners they had all been looking for.

A member of the armed response unit spoke to him, "The rest of the house is clear Guv, you wanna go look downstairs." Ford looked at him, and then back at the bodies. He turned to walk out of the room, glanced to the stairs leading down. His legs wobbled, "Get it to-fucking-gether prick," he shouted in his own head. He descended down the wooden steps. At the bottom was a metal door, on the bottom step a discarded padlock with the key in it. The door was wide open. As he stepped into the room he looked around.

The room itself about twenty feet long by ten feet. Bare block walls. He glanced down at the floor, a large dark red puddle about three feet across, and another a few feet from it. Over by the wall, two gurneys with handcuffs hanging from them. One was clean, the other covered in blood. On the wall in front of him were several dark red stains and there were more on the floor.

"This is where he had them, fuck, we missed him." He thought. He walked over to the ledge that Malcolm had used to rest his trays of water, and leant on it, hands on his thighs, head down. "Fuck," he thought again. As he leaned there Ash walked down the stairs and into the room.

"There are fresh tyre tracks in a mud patch on the rear driveway, forensics are all over it. I spoke with the neighbour that called the letting agent's emergency number at 3am this morning. She quotes the van left at some point around 10pm, returned around 10.30pm which gives him enough time to drop of Chris, and then she quotes some noise around midnight and the van drove away again about 2.30am." He put the notepad he was referring to away. "I went up to the room she said she could see the van, I'm pretty sure she would only have been able to see the roof, and probably couldn't see what was getting loaded."

"The bodies?" Ford nodded upstairs.

"Forensics are in the room. I'm confident it's the family that lived here, the Alderman's. They've been here six months according to the letting agent, quiet tenants according to the neighbour I spoke with." Ash was referring to his notes again, he hated this, being the bearer of bad news, and they had gotten so close. On the way here his adrenaline was pumping thinking he was going to get the son of a bitch.

"I want their backstories," Ford said coming to his senses. He had work to do, and his work just got harder and more complicated. "I need to go and see MacHray, she's going to fucking love this." The sarcasm was clear in his voice. "Why fucking kill them all, how is that linked to this game he is playing?" Ash sensed his question was rhetorical at this stage, but certainly a question they would need to answer back at the Yard. Ford looked at his watch. Just before 8. "I'm heading in, get what you can here and let forensics do the rest, you and Burnham back at the Yard pronto. We've still got a deadline."

He climbed the stairs, glanced at the room with the bodies, it was filled with forensics in white overalls. He walked out the front door and stood on the top step. As he looked around the media had already caught the story and were visible beyond the blue tape about two hundred yards away. There was an ambulance, seven police cars, and a mobile incident centre was just pulling up. He walked back to his car, leaving Ash to dish out instructions to the team.

As he drove away from the scene he dialled Burnham first.

"Boss, what a shit storm," Burnham announced, "I've spoken to the boy, not much he can say, grief-stricken at the moment. Described the cellar to me, but I suppose that's not relevant now we're there. I'm heading to the Yard, I'm assuming you are too?"

"Yes, you head straight to the Ops Room, Ash will meet you there soon. Start compiling information about the family we've just found as it might create a lead, but I think the focus still needs to be his current location." Ford pulled up at a set of lights, "I'll go see MacHray, she'll need to see the media again, and they will have a field day." He continued on his way when the light turned green. "Every other property he's been at, I want them all searched, by warrant if we have to, and I want it done by lunchtime. I just hope there is no one else wrapped in plastic." With that, he hung up.

October, 2015

Malcolm sat and watched the husband and wife walk up the front stairs with the letting agent. From inside his little Fiesta, he took photos on his phone, zooming in as close as he could to their faces. As the three disappeared inside he waited patiently, pouring black coffee from his flask into the plastic cup that doubled as its lid. For about twenty minutes he sat in his car, scanning the pictures of the interior house on the letting agent's website. He scanned through pictures of the bedrooms, the kitchen and saw the picture of the basement. It was perfect. He glanced up as the front door finally opened and the three stepped outside into the fresh October air again. Shaking hands with the letting agent, they descended the stone stairs and returned to their cars before leaving.

He thumbed through the photos on his phone quickly, checking out pictures of Darren and his new wife on Facebook. Placing his finger on the button on the door handle he waited for the window to lower before discarding the dregs of his coffee onto the street. As he pulled to the end of the street he could see the couple at the following junction. He pulled in behind them and followed them through London for about twenty minutes until they arrived at a well-presented semi-detached house in the suburbs.

The couple parked on the drive behind a new Volvo saloon and as they started to get out of the car the front door opened. A silver-haired woman stepped out into the front garden, her eyes wide with questions, and clearly the answer given by her son was the one she wanted to hear. Bringing her son in for a hug she beckoned for the daughter-in-law to join the embrace. Moments later a bald man stepped out of the front door, with three small children, two girls, and a boy, rushing past them. They were all smiling, the news of the new property must have been one they were all excited about. Malcolm sat across the street taking pictures, the children looked to be aged between three and ten years old, Darren and his wife in their late thirties, starting out on life together.

After the hugs in the front garden, the family stepped inside the house. Malcolm poured another coffee and reclined his seat slightly. He was getting patient at this waiting game. He used his time to find out about the wife on social media, Susan Navin, mother of two teenage boys. It was clear the two had left their significant others for each other, they had been together a while now according to their feeds, celebrating decisions to move in together some months back. About an hour went by when Susan stepped out of the house on her own. She climbed into the driver's seat, adjusted the chair and reversed out of the drive, with Malcolm starting his ignition and following her through London. After about half an hour she pulled into the carpark of a McDonalds, parking her car and walking inside. Malcolm reverse parked into a bay and went inside. As he walked in through the sliding door the woman was directly in front of him in the queue, she waited her turn and ordered a coffee from the teenager at the register, moving over to a seat by the window. Malcolm ordered a Big Mac and waited for a few moments for it to be placed on a tray, he spotted a table a few seats away from the woman and took a seat.

From his position he could see Susan, sitting hunched forward, both hands clasping her cup. She had not removed her scarf or her woollen hat but sat staring at the door. Malcolm was halfway through his burger when two boys entered the door with a man. Spotting his ex-wife, the man spoke briefly to the boys, teenagers, wearing hoodies and jeans, they walked over to Susan whilst the man went to order food.

Malcolm sat watching the family out of the corner of his eye, listening to the parts of the conversation he could hear. The conversation looked difficult, Susan was trying not to cry as the man joined them with burgers and fries for the boys and a coffee for himself. She explained that she had just signed the lease on a new property so they could come and stay with her. There was some chat about the man's work offshore, but it was clear the boys did not want to go and visit. Although consoling them, their Dad was clear that they needed to go so he could work, otherwise, he would need to give up their home as well. Malcolm could tell that the boys were respectful but upset at the situation. Finishing his burger he left the restaurant and returned to his car, sitting patiently, waiting for the woman to leave.

Wednesday, April 12th

The shipping container Malcolm had moved his prisoners too was a lot more cramped than the cellar, longer but narrow. It was on the edge of an industrial complex, plenty of shipping containers that were used for storage for all sorts of reasons, from tradesmen to people moving home. On the inside of the container, Malcolm had framed it and installed soundproofing boards to minimize the noise from inside. This made the inside slightly narrower than eight feet, but with it being thirty feet in length he could fit all of the gurneys snuggly.

The night before, as he was leaving with Chris, he had noticed the curtains of the neighbouring property twitching, and with the dog walker looking directly at him, he decided he needed to enforce his backup plan. Although he was a strong man, lifting the five unconscious bodies and their gurneys, up the stairs and into the back of the van, and then from there into the container, was exhausting but necessary work. The container was a suitable new home for his prisoners. When he installed the soundproofing he had tested it by playing loudspeakers from within, and it proved effective.

As the five began to wake up from there enforced sleep, the same reactions unfolded as had done when they came round for the first time in the cellar. Malcolm was now limited to where he could go during the day. He had several hoodies, sunglasses, and even a pretty realistic wig, but he didn't want to take any chances, so he sat in the corner of the container just waiting. With him, he had a couple of iPads, a stack of burner phones, and a video camera. Everything he needed to make his videos.

He pressed record and began to speak.

"Well, well, well people of Great Britain. What a nice surprise last night. Mrs. Johnstone made the ultimate sacrifice for her son and even gave a little speech to the media. Now we have two ways we can look at the outcome. Firstly, Mrs. Johnstone is a devoted mother and no matter what happens she put her child first. Chris, her son, can now grow up learning about his mother's sacrifice and change his life for the better, and hopefully become an upstanding member of society. Or, and this needs some serious consideration, Chris is that messed up that he will spiral out of control. Maybe his taste for young girls will overtake any morality he may have left, and possibly Mrs. Johnstone has just created a prolific sex offender. Who knows? But is the world a better place with Chris in it? Anyway, it was quite a show, I hope you'll agree.

"Now onto tonight. I may as well tell you about Harry Kalarahi. You see, he looks after his Dad who is seventy-five and suffers from Alzheimer's. He is his doting carer, he has given up his life to look after his Dad ... a noble thing, yes? Well, that's what he tells his friends and family, when in fact he lives off his father's disability cheques and his hefty pension, while his father lives in filth and squalor and gets handcuffed to a radiator every time he leaves the property. So, it will be interesting to see what this upstanding member of society does at 9pm tonight. I'll certainly be tuned in, I hope you will be too."

He stopped the recording, placing his iPad in its case, and spent some time on an editing suite making sure the audio played well. He then grabbed one of the burner phones. He put his sunglasses on and pulled the hood over his head. Glancing through a small hole he had made in the door, he checked outside, no one in sight. He opened the door enough to slide out, and then banged it closed, dropping the catch and feeding a heavy chain through the loops. Fixing with a padlock he pulled from his pocket, he then walked off in the direction of the entrance to the yard.

As he walked a couple of streets he pulled a car key out of his pocket and climbed into a small ford fiesta. The sun was out so at least he wouldn't look at odds on this April day as he began driving through London. He didn't know much about how the police could track signals through mobile phones, but he just figured that if the phone was brand new, not registered to anyone, and then destroyed after, they would be unable to trace him. After about a half-hour drive he pulled over to a side street. Looking around it was quiet, so he unboxed the burner and switched it on after inserting a SIM. He synced the phone to the iPad and transferred the video to the burner. Logging on to his YouTube account he uploaded the video from the burner, switched it off, removed the SIM card. Just behind him on the path was a waste bin, he briefly got out of the car and threw the phone and packaging in the bin before returning to his seat and closing the door. He drove in the direction he had come.

As he arrived back at the container, the yard was still quiet. He parked his car alongside the container and went to the boot. From there he collected a box full of water and snacks, a sleeping bag which he slung over his shoulder and a small portable heater. Placing these outside the door of the container he listened again, no sound could be heard from within which pleased him. He trotted back to the Fiesta and closed the boot, before returning to unlock the bolt and chain.

As he entered the container as quickly as he could, five pairs of eyes were looking at him, and he heard the groans and cries from behind the gags he had become accustomed too. Closing the door he then threaded the chained and padlocked it from the inside. Should he be found he wanted to make sure that his prisoners did not leave the container alive.

Wednesday, April 12th 11am

As Ford sat in the chair opposite MacHray, they stared at each other for a few moments without saying anything. Both of them knew how much shit they were in. "What do we know about the family, Jim?" MacHray asked looking at her watch, "In an hour I'm in front of the cameras again, the media are looking for blood, my superiors are screaming down my neck. They are wanting heads," she paused, looking directly at Ford, "but I'm not giving them anyone, Jim."

Ford paused, he needed to be professional, cast any thought of the effect this case could have on him or his career. "They were called the Alderman's, Husband and Wife, she had two sons from a previous marriage, he had three, two daughters and a son. Both were working parents. Both left significant others a year or so ago, moved into the house a few months ago." A flash of the bodies piled up struck Ford's mind and he made a slight wince, "Initial examination at the scene seems to suggest some torture. The three youngest children killed with a knife to the throat, the two teenagers stabbed in the abdomen. The woman may have been raped before her throat was cut, and the man butchered, stabbed in excess of twenty times. They are in the process of being removed from the property, they'll be in our morgue soon." He paused again, thinking about his next words carefully, "I don't want to transfer any resources to that part of the investigation, it's not worth it."

"Excuse me, Jim, did I just hear you right?" she said with a vein of distaste in her mouth. She knew Ford very well, but her instant reaction to what he had just requested jolted her.

"They're dead, Ma'am, and investigating it right now won't change a dam thing." He took a sigh, forcing his mind to stay away from the pile of dead bodies, "Its 11am, in ten hours I have to try and save Harry's Dad, and I currently have nothing. We were so close, just a few hours behind him. He's got another lair, we just have to find it."

MacHray sat back in her seat, "What do I tell the press, and my bosses?" she asked with disdain on her face.

"Just what we know, the facts, Malcolm used this property, probably because of its basement, the family probably unlucky house guests. He has murdered this family to gain access to the basement to carry out this game. Don't mention anything about torture." He stood up, "tell the press this guy is a psycho if you have to. Frankly, they'll make their own stories up anyway. I'm sorry Ma'am, I need to get back down to the Ops Room and review what we've got." With a brief nod of her head, Ford left the room. MacHray, not for the first time this week, hated her job.

When Ford returned to the Ops Room, Chilton was just taking off his jacket, Burnham was pinning pictures of the family to the board. "Forget them for now," Ford barked, Burnham, Chilton and the rest of the detectives stopped what they were doing. "Listen up. This shit has gone drastically sideways and I'm sick of it, as I am sure you all are. The family we found today will not help us find Malcolm, we need to prioritise if we are going to save more people. When we catch Malcolm, and by Christ we will, he'll pay for what he has done. But we still have five innocent people out there, and five innocent people in here." He looked around the room, twenty officers were all focussed on him, "I don't need to tell you all how to do your jobs, you are all fucking good at them, but we need to rattle every cage, knock on every door, look under every hedgerow if we are going to find this fucker. I don't need to know why he is doing it, I don't need a lesson in the morality of the people involved, what I need is you all to get out with uniform and find this mother fucker before tonight!" His voice was getting louder and louder, as he finished speaking the men stood staring, "MOVE!!!"

Each officer in the room, besides Chilton and Burnham, began picking up coats and notepads from various desks and chairs and began moving out the door. Ford turned to his team.

"Boss, all the houses have been checked," said Burnham, "all residents living and accounted for. He isn't holed up in one of his old haunts."

"Malcolm's bank records run dry about eighteen months ago when he left Serpio," Chilton piped up, "seems he has been running off cash since then, probably has some off the books work. We have three shop keepers that have reported Malcolm being a regular customer over the past year."

"Get men near those shops," said Ford, "make sure they are discreet not sitting in cars across the street."

"If he hasn't used one of his previous properties to go to, then he must be somewhere big enough to put five people in gurneys," Burnham had walked back over to the map. "He's a homeboy, lived around this area all his life, he'll know the back alleys, the side streets, he won't want to go far."

Ford and Chilton joined him, "So he needs to leave wherever he is hiding every time he posts a video, we don't have any reports of the van other than last night, so that must be stationary most of the time. He's got another vehicle." Chilton was talking more out loud but as he spoke he began to form some ideas, "he's been using these three shops," he pulled three spare pins from the top of the board and focussed on the map to pinpoint the shops, "and he drank in this pub a lot, this area covers about twenty streets. I say we focus here," tapping his finger on the map he looked at Ford, "we go door to door, check back gardens and garages. We should centre here and work out. When we go door to door we check basements as well."

"What else have we got?" asked Ford without wanting a reply, "Centre as many uniforms and Detectives as possible around that area, everyone wears stab vests, that means you two as well if you're out and about, this guy likes his knives. You two stay here, control the op, I've got to speak to our Sikh friend." Ford left the room.

As he entered the room where Harry Kalarahi had been bunked, the man looked up from a newspaper he was reading. "Wondered when you would turn up," he said to Ford without looking up. "Time for a big speech is it?"

"Listen, Harry," Ford pulled up a chair and sat close to Harry, leaning forward so his face was about two feet away, "This is not the big speech moment, I'm not wasting my breath, but you need to understand how your life is going to be after tonight. Every self-righteous thug in London will be looking for you, every vigilante looking to make a name for himself down the pub, and if I can pin a case on you, and you better believe I will, I know a few inmates who owe me favours if I can get you inside as well." Ford was sinister, it was just the two of them, he didn't care what Harry said outside this room, he'd deny it all and would be believed. "You better believe that one way or another you'll pay for what you've done to your Dad." With that, he stood up and walked to the door. He looked back before he opened it "I'll see you at 8pm, because one way or another, you're sitting in that chair."

As he pulled the handle on the door Harry spoke, "You know what copper, you sound just like that guy Malcolm." Jim didn't look back again, he just left the room.

August, 1995

The knock on the door was the last of his shift. Malcolm held his toolbox in his left hand and a job sheet in his right hand. The job with the council was a decent one, paid minimum wage but it was relatively easy. He was a general handyman employed to work on small repair jobs. This was the last of five he was scheduled to do today, looking down at the slip he smirked as it only said "SILICONE REPAIR" which, if it was true, would be an easy end to his day.

After a few moments, the chain was released on the door and a man with a turban stood in front of him, around thirty years old. "Council mate," Malcolm offered his introduction.

"Yeah, about time," replied the man, "I've been waiting in all day for you." He stood to the side, allowing Malcolm to step into the hallway.

"Well I'm here now," stated Malcolm. He hated this type of tenant, acting like they are so inconvenienced having to wait in for things to be fixed. The guy's tone of voice meant this could be a chore of a job. "Mr. Kalarahi?"

"Yeah, Harry," he walked passed Malcolm, heading for the stairs, "it's the upstairs bathroom, bloody leaking into my kitchen." As they climbed the stairs Malcolm couldn't help but look at the state of the place. He walked on an orange and black carpet, a few patches where it had worn thin, wood panelling lined the whole of the staircase, yellow stains on the ceiling, the painted handrail more yellow than white.

At the top of the stairs, Harry opened the first door which led into a small bathroom. "All yours mate," Harry grunted and headed back down the stairs. As he got about three steps down he turned back. "Hey, don't go in that room," he gestured to the next door along, "my pops is asleep."

"Sure," Malcolm agreed, stepping into the bathroom. Watching the Asian man descend the rest of the staircase he shook his head at the man's ignorance and turned to work. Looking at the bath he could see the issue straight away, the silicone around the bath seal was old, meaning water could seep down through the gap. He set his tool bag down and removed a Stanley knife from it. Running the blade around the edge of the bath he began to pull the loose silicone away, stretching it until it snapped. After a few minutes the vast majority of it was cleared, then taking a caulking gun from his bag and a tube of silicone he set about running a smooth line around the rim, creating a good seal. The whole job only took about ten minutes as he started clearing his tools away.

Malcolm could hear the guy Harry on his phone downstairs, shouting at someone, and from what he could make out he was arranging a collection of dope. He was about to pick up his tool bag after collecting the old bits of silicone and placing them in the bathroom waste bin, when he heard the guy's father in the next room coughing and looking down the staircase there was no apparent movement from the son to come to his aid.

He walked along the short corridor to the next door, noticing the key in the lock, on the outside of the door. He turned the handle and the door failed to move, lowering his hand to the key he turned it slowly, the click of the lock releasing the door. Malcolm paused to listen for the man downstairs, hearing him still organising his drugs, and he slowly opened the door.

The smell hit him hard, sulphur went right up his nose and burnt his sinuses. His hand instantly caught over his mouth, pinching his nose. Behind the door, the room was dark, although it was daylight outside. A stained sheet was hung at the window, and as his gaze scanned the room he saw the old man on a bed. It was metal framed and basic, the mattress he lay on looked like it was just an inch thick, and a brown blanket covered part of his body. The man lay with striped pyjama bottoms on but his torso was bare. As Malcolm continued to look into the gloom he noticed that both of the man's wrists were handcuffed to the metal bed head. The old man's hair, long and seemingly matted, his skin covered in bruises, visible even in the dull light. He was mumbling, but not anything that Malcolm could understand.

Malcolm was frozen in the doorway, he wanted to help the poor man, and he wanted to go and confront the son, Harry, and ask him what the hell was going on. Maybe, he thought, he should just phone social services. He thought briefly about his options. Helping the man would mean confronting the son, and he knew that would not work out well, he needed his job and didn't want the guy to report him for snooping around the house. He thought about social services, but his own experiences there meant that was pretty pointless. Looking at the man he turned and left the room, closing the door quietly, turning the key, and picking up his tool bag from the entrance to the bathroom where he had left it.

He reached the bottom of the stairs and gave the slip to Harry, who was still on the phone, Harry signed the bottom and went back to his conversation. Malcolm left without saying a word.

Wednesday, April 12th, 2pm

Jim walked down the hospital corridor, he spotted the officer outside the room that Chris Johnstone was in. As he entered the room, a nurse was finishing off taking his vitals. She looked at Jim "Not too long, he still needs rest," Jim nodded at her as she issued her order.

"Chris, I'm DCI Jim Ford." He introduced himself.

"You were with my Mum," Chris answered with a quiet voice. The young man was white with shock, and close to tears again. "I saw you on the TV."

Jim gestured to a chair, asking permission to sit, Chris nodded. "I spent some time with your mother before she died. She was a good woman, and a good mother." Chris turned his face away from Jim.

"I thought I was dead," he said, "I lay in that basement and I thought my mum wouldn't even show. I thought that man was going to come and kill me." The tears could be heard now, Chris was trying to be a brave man, but his adolescence was betraying him. "And then she showed up, and spoke to the cameras, and sat in the …" he didn't finish his sentence.

Jim sat quietly for a moment, considering his next words. "It was an easy decision for your mum to make."

Chris turned back to face Jim, his eyes glared at him, "She should have killed me, I would have."

"Your mother loved you, Chris, right to the very end. She wants you to live, to make the most of a life that has not been easy for you." Jim leaned forward, his bedside manner had not always been very good, but he was making a conscious effort to make this young man feel like he was worth something. "Your Mum told me about you. You're a lad that's made a mistake, and you have never come to terms with it. You have a chance to make her proud Chris, that's what she wanted for you, and if I can help, I will." He reached into his jacket pocket and pulled out the envelope Nicola had given to him and passed it to Chris, "Your mother asked me to give this to you. She made the ultimate sacrifice so you could make the most of your life. It's up to you what you do with it."

With that, Jim got up and left the room.

February, 2016

Malcolm sat outside the house that the Alderman's lived in. He had sat there on many occasions over the past few weeks, watching the family come and go, noting down times and watching for patterns.

It had been a month since the couple with the five children had moved in and he had sat and watched them quite frequently since the day they moved in. On that day several vans and car loads of furniture and boxes had been hauled up the front stairs, along with visitors including the parents he had seen at the semi-detached in the suburbs.

He scanned through his notepad, considering he knew enough about the family by now and placed it on the passenger seat as he started the engine. Once he had driven back to his lock-up, he parked outside, lifting his hoodie to shield his face, checking to make sure no one was watching before stepping out of his car and unbolting the door to the container. Pulling the heavy door open he stepped inside and slammed it shut, switching on the light over the makeshift desk. In the corner of the metal container was a blow-up mattress and a sleeping bag, and seven collapsed gurneys stacked in the middle in two piles. Most of the interior had been framed and sheeted, with a couple of panels left to be screwed to the ceiling and the wall.

Malcolm pulled up a wooden stool and began thumbing through his notepad, re-reading all the information he could about the family. "Mr. and Mrs. Alderman," he said out loud, "nice to meet you." He picked up a tablet and unplugged the charger, flipping to Facebook and clicking on his most recent search of their names. It wasn't long before he found their pictures and began linking the pieces of their lives together. He knew Darren, and over the last few months had gotten to know Susan Navin in a lot of detail, dates of birth, linking to their children and finding out information about them, her ex-husband, his ex-wife, where they worked, what their hobbies were. He wrote as much as possible down and kept up to date with their day to day posts.

By the time he had finished, he knew a lot about this couple. They had both been married previously but reading between the lines of social media posts had started an affair before being caught by their respective others. Darren's ex-wife was the one that seemed to be a lot more vocal on Facebook, actively spending a few months posting about how she had found out and how devastated she was. Susan's ex was a lot quieter, generally posting pictures of his boys, or leaving posts about when he was headed offshore.

Several hours past whilst Malcolm was doing his homework, with the occasional break to fill the kettle from a water bottle in the corner to make himself a coffee. Once he felt he had enough, he closed his note pad and looked to the sound boarding sheets in the corner. Walking over to his drill he lifted it up and set to work finishing off his lair.

Wednesday, April 12th, 4pm

For the rest of the day, Jim spent it in the Ops Room with Ash and Brad, co-ordinating searches, updating the board and liaising with the Forensics team. They were never quiet but the clock up on the wall had a deafening tick from the second hand. Their teams were coming up with nothing, door to door searches were slow and painful as every outhouse and shed of considerable size was being searched. They had some leads on stolen white vans from other parts of the country that could well be the vehicle he was using, but even that didn't help them locate Malcolm. The clock was ticking and it appeared Malcolm was beating them.

"Expand the search," Jim announced standing up straight, stretching his lower back. He had been stood leaning over at a desk for too long looking at Malcolm's bank records. There was very little in them, the guy drew cash and spent it, only his utility bills were paid by direct debit, but even those had ceased over two years ago. He walked over to the board, "Get me the locations of these cash machines, there's more than one that he was using." He picked up a pin, located a road on the map that had some shops on it within the current search area, "this street here is the only cash machine I am aware of local to where we are searching. Looking at his bank statements, he used three others on a regular basis. Let's find out where they are and start knocking doors." With that, Brad picked up an iPad and one of the sheets from the bank statements and started searching. It was thin and a big gamble as the bank account had been idle for so long, but it widened the search area, although spreading resources.

Looking around at all the other pieces of paper on the desk, "I want a blue pin in all the confirmed sightings of Malcolm and red pin in the possibles." Ash got to work, rubbing his eyes as they went which did not go unnoticed by Jim. Brad poured some coffee and lifted a desk phone that was ringing. It was the morgue and the medical officer advising the Alderman family had arrived. He spoke for a few moments before hanging up and returning to the table.

"Boss, that's the morgue, they are beginning to process the family, they'll update with anything relevant." He advised.

"Anything new from the house?" Asked Jim, predicting the answer.

"Nothing boss, Malcolm is not hiding from us." Ash replied, interrupting Brad, "We know his face, he has no reason to worry about fingerprints or DNA, and there is nothing but microwave meals and pot noodles in the house." Ash pulled out a seat and sat down looking at Jim. "We're running a blank Jim, he is a man who has lived off the grid for the last few years, and we are truly hoping for a lucky break.

"What's Harry saying to it?" Brad pulled out another chair and sat next to Ash.

A long sigh drew from Jim's mouth, "That prick is why Malcolm is doing this. He knows the old man is dead already, he knows the British public is watching and will expect to see blood on the pavement after the video he played this morning." He leant forward, arms folded on the table, "and the prick knows the British public will want blood if they don't see it."

The rest of the afternoon involved phone calls from the officers on the street, forensics offering dead ends, and sifting through dozens of calls into the hotlines.

March, 2003

The light from the hallway broke into the room as Harry turned the handle of the door with his left hand and pushed it open. In his right hand a tray with a plate and a glass of water. On the plate was a sandwich with a slice of cheese and two rich tea biscuits. He placed the tray on the small side table next to the bed and sat down on the edge of the mattress next to his father.

"Time for you to eat," he said to his father, leaning over him with a key between his fingers and unlocking the handcuff from his right wrist. The old man looked at him with wide eyes as his arm was freed.

"Rizwan, my son," the frail voice spoke towards this man that sat on his bed, "it's so good to see you."

"Whatever pops," Harry placed his big hands under the armpits of his father and lifted him upright in the bed so he was sitting upright. He took the plate with the cheese sandwich on it and placed it on his father's lap. The old man looked at it, picked it up with his free hand and took a bite. Chewing it slowly and crumbs fell down his chin and onto his chest.

The room was practically bare. The metal-framed bed sat on wooden floorboards, a two-inch think mattress on top of the wire frame, a blanket, and a pillow provided the only comfort for the old man. At the window a black sheet was nailed around the frame, hanging down in the middle allowing shards of daylight to reflect off the ceiling. The table next to the bed was basic and a sparse lightbulb dangled from the ceiling. To the left of the bed, opposite the window was an old steel radiator, and at the base lay a metal chain.

The old man swallowed his mouthful of sandwich and Harry leant over for the glass of water, lifting it to his father's mouth allowing him to take a few sips. His father's eyes squinted at him in the shadowy room, "Rizwan, my son, it's good to see you."

His son got up from the bed, "You stupid old man," he grunted as he walked to the radiator, "I'm Harry, Rizwan is dead." His words were harsh and tears formed in the eyes of the old man as he heard them. Harry leant down and picked up the chain, and a padlock that was sitting next to it, dragging it over to the bed as it rattled off the floorboards and then clanked of the metal frame of the bed. "I'm going out so eat your sandwich and don't fuck around." He wrapped the chain around his father's ankle, ignoring the blue bruises that were already there, and fastened it with the padlock.

As he walked to the door he looked back at his father lying in the bed, staring back at him with tears on his cheeks. "If you need a piss use the bucket this time, I'm sick of cleaning you." With that he walked out into the hallway, closing the door behind him and turning a key in the Chubb lock.

In the darkness, the man sobbed. He rolled over onto his side knocking the plate and barely touched sandwich onto the floor, the plate shattering and the noise making him jump under the blanket. He was confused, the man in the room was his son Rizwan, but the man said Rizwan was dead. It didn't make sense, and the more he tried to make sense of it the more upset he got. He knew something was wrong with himself, he had these moments of dread where things got confusing and that caused him to panic. His eyes scanned the chain on the radiator, and he wondered why his beloved son would chain him up.

He closed his eyes and wiped a sleeve of his pyjamas against them, dampening the cloth. He was concentrating on a memory of Rizwan, trying not to let it go into the murk of his diseased brain. Rizzie was his baby, but the memory was of him in a hospital bed, he remembered kissing him on the forehead, but the scary realisation was that his son was already dead as he kissed him. The man sobbed, as the memory faded.

Wednesday, April 12th, 8pm

At 8pm Jim opened the door and looked at Harry. Harry rose to his feet instantly. "Shall we do this then?" The nonchalant attitude of Harry sickened Jim to his stomach, the type of criminal that the police were just too ill-equipped to deal with, and the type of criminal that inspired Malcolm to begin his game.

Ash and Brad were waiting by the car, they opened the back door to the BMW and allowed Harry to step in, Brad was driving with Ash climbing into the passenger seat, and Jim joining Harry in the back. As they drove Jim began to speak to Harry. "How long has he suffered from dementia Harry?"

The man looked back at Jim, a permanent frown formed on Harry's face that reminded Jim of a bratty teenager. "About twenty-five years." His answer was blunt, telling Jim he didn't want to talk.

"So for twenty-five years, you've been keeping him locked in that bedroom?" Jim looked at Harry who looked straight ahead, fixing his gaze on the back of Ash's headrest. Jim decided to take a different approach. "You know, when you get home tonight, we'll offer some protection, maybe a couple of uniforms parked outside … " Ash pulled up at a set of lights, they weren't in a rush so he was taking the scenic route for Jim, "that protection might be there for a couple of days, but with budgets and prioritisation, it will be removed quite quickly. There will be people in the crowd tonight that won't forget, that won't need to see facts and evidence, they'll have your number marked tonight." Ash pulled off from the lights, they were about two minutes away from the Square. Harry was not flinching, this sanctimonious piece of shit was like concrete.

As the lights flickered above the car, Ash pulled into the square, driving slowly through the crowd of police vehicles and officers. There were visibly more people here tonight. "Nicola's suicide has brought out the vultures," Jim said to Ash and Brad as they stepped out of the car. Ash opened the rear door and Harry stepped out, and as he came into view of the crowd the noise level increased dramatically. The shouts, chants, and screams were almost too much to bare. Jim looked over at Harry, for the first time in a while Harry caught his gaze. Although Jim did not care for the man stood looking back at him, he believed in the justice system, and what Malcolm had orchestrated was a trap that had little to do with the legal system. He glanced at his watch, 8.57.

"It's time," said Jim, "even if you aren't going to pull the trigger, the least you could do is sit in the damn chair, so everyone can see you condemn your father to death." He spoke mean, he looked mean.

"And what about you detective," Harry's use of the word detective was slow and sarcastic, "there is a man out there making you all look like fools, and you're playing his game." With that, he walked away from the car in the direction of the chair. As he walked he began to swag, like he was some sort of gangster rapper in a music video. He raised his arms above his head as he walked, pumping his hands as if he was some sort of celebrity riling up an audience. He reached the chair, spinning around slowly so everyone could see him, arms out wide, peacocking for the cameras. He glanced down at the gun, picked it up. For the briefest of moments, Jim thought he would do it, looking on from his vantage point at the parked BMW, standing next to Ash and Brad. Harry heard the first chime of Big Ben, put the gun in his mouth … and then paused, his mouth forming a grin around the barrel.

As he removed the gun from his mouth he raised it into the air, pointing it upwards, the three detectives could hear his fake, sarcastic laughter, and the kind that this depraved human being delivered when he felt he was above the law. Harry pulled the trigger, cracking the bullet into the sky, and dropped the gun back onto the chair. Jim stood silent for a second, Harry turned to look at him. "FUCK YOU, PIG!" Harry shouted at the top of his lungs.

The shouts from the crowd were angry, about ten feet from Harry a bottle smashed on the ground, catching his attention. Then another a few feet from it. Harry stepped back a couple of feet, as a third bottle smashed against his forehead. Bottles and stones began to land all around him as a section of the crowd began to push against the riot police. The three detectives began to run toward Harry, and he moved towards them, clasping his head as blood seeped through his fingers. Reaching Harry, the detectives instinctively formed a sort of shield around him and as the four made it back to the car they climbed in. "MOVE" shouted Jim, as Ash started the ignition and accelerated from the scene, leaving a riot forming behind them.

Wednesday, April 12th, 9.05pm

In the darkness of the container, the shadows cast out by the iPad flickered across the eyes of the captive audience. The BBC coverage had shown the callous charade delivered by the old man's son and now showed the riot police battling against a large crowd of angry spectators, high above from the safety of a news camera in a helicopter. In his chair, Malcolm watched the screen, it had been five minutes since Harry fired his pistol into the air which had caused a muffled commotion from his guests.

As the news replayed the scene with headlines scrolling along the bottom, he leaned over to his DIY shelf and picked up the twelve-inch blade. "Predictable," he said aloud, "The British public is made up of characters like your relatives, people who forgot what it takes to be decent. Harry, there was absolutely no surprise, I knew he was the kind of character to not give a dam about anyone but himself. And as I predicted, with the British public, you sit like a tinder box waiting to go up in flames, only requiring a little spark to start the inferno." He turned to look at the gurneys and began walking towards them. Harry's Dad was closest to him, he was crying, he was in a lucid state and his eyes remained fixed on the small screen on the shelf.

"That's my boy," said the frail old man, tears on his cheeks but a smile on his face. Malcolm placed the blade on the left jugular, dug it in deep, and slid it to the right. The gurgling sound was deafened by the muted screams from the remaining hostages. As the life drained from his neck he remained fixed on the screen, looking at his son, arms in the air, smiling at him as the light dimmed and his body went limp.

Malcolm took his time cleaning off the knife, ignoring the cries and whimpers. He removed a key from his pocket and unlocked the handcuffs around the wrists of the man he had just murdered. Returning to the corner of the container he picked up the roll of clear sheeting and began laying it on the floor, before lifting Mr. Kalarahi onto it and wrapping him up as he had done with other bodies many times before. He looked through the spyhole of the front door before considering opening it, seeing the courtyard in front was empty he carefully unlocked the chain, taking care to go slowly to minimise the noise as he pushed the door. Walking to the Fiesta he opened the back doors and dropped the rear seats, and then moved to the boot and opened it. He figured the police would be looking for the van by now, using the car was more of a squeeze for the body, but it was essential.

Returning to the body in the container, he picked it up and hoisted it over his shoulder. Looking at the four remaining guests, all eyes were fixed on him, he grinned and walked back to the car, dumping the body unceremoniously in the boot so it was in the foetal position. One final walk back to push the heavy door closed, he chained it and set off in the car. His drive was about fifteen minutes along back roads and side streets, again finding a quiet place without prying eyes to drop the body and the return home to the container.

Wednesday, April 12th, 10pm

"Book this prick," Jim instructed the desk sergeant, "I read him his rights, benefit fraud, abuse, I'll do the paperwork in the morning." Even with that Harry stood tall, a snarl on his top lip, his defiance of the situation pissed Jim off and Jim was angry. As the desk sergeant took over, Jim went outside where Ash and Brad were waiting, Brad, offering a cigarette. He knew Jim didn't smoke often, but he also knew he'd take one tonight.

"Shitty boss, real fucking shitty," said Ash, "our own fucking system just got that poor old guy killed." He leant against the wall at the entrance of the carpark, puffing on his e-cig.

Brad leant next to him. "They are rioting all over London, Birmingham, Bradford, Manchester, and Newcastle." He drew the last draw of his smoke as it singed the butt and then stubbed it out on the metal ashtray on the wall.

Jim did the same and turned to his two detectives. "Go home guys, I don't want you in before eight tomorrow. Mr. Kalarahi will be found, we'll speak to Claire first thing and consider our options." He puffed out the last breath of smoke. "I'm going home." With that, he turned and headed to his car.

Ash walked to his car, dug his keys out and pressed the button. He glanced over at Brad opening the door of his own car as they caught each other's gaze they gave each other a quick nod. He climbed in and started the engine, driving to the entrance and turning onto the main road. As his car connected to his Bluetooth, he used the steering wheel buttons to call his girlfriend.

"Hey babes, you ok?" she answered. Ash had been dating Lisa for three years. She was a Canadian born artist and they had met through friends, instantly hitting it off. After moving in together a year later they decided to become a family and she was currently expecting their first child. She had been concerned for him all day and it showed in her voice.

"It's been a tough one, baby, Jim has taken it hard. Did you watch?"

"Yes, I had to, and I am so sorry. This guy is a real psycho," she paused, "you're not ok are you?"

Ash was holding it together in front of the guys, but with Lisa, he felt his emotions pulling to the surface. "I will be," the lump in his throat was audible, "I just need to see you and little bump and I'll be fine."

"Well you know where I am," she replied, "how long will you be?"

"The roads are quiet, I've just left."

"See you in twenty, I'll make us a brew, love you," with that she disconnected.

Friday, April 7th, 4pm

Susan answered the front door after hanging up on Darren, he had just called to advise that he would be home and she'd asked him to pick up some peppers to go with the fajitas she was planning on making. The kids were all upstairs in their rooms but it would soon be tea time and a hungry brood of five children needed appeasing. The past couple of months living in the new house had seemed to settle them, especially her two boys who had been the most upset following the family breakups. They were more comfortable to stay over while her ex-husband was on the rigs, and although she hadn't seen them in two weeks, when they arrived yesterday they had tried their best to make it a pleasant exchange.

She still had the phone in her hand as the door opened, she looked briefly at the big set man standing on the doorstep, a hood covering his head and eyes, a rucksack on his shoulder. The swift movement of his arm and his lunge forward caught her completely by surprise, and as the tazer connected with her, the shock of electricity made her yelp as she collapsed to the floor. Stepping inside Malcolm quickly closed the door and listened for noise within the property. He had been watching all day, he knew the kids were all here but Darren was not home from work yet. Placing the tazer in the pocket of his hoodie, he stepped around her slumped body and grabbed her under the arms dragging her to the door under the stairs. Turning the handle and opening the door, he lifted her up onto his shoulder and climbed down the stairs, opening the metal door at the bottom. Looking at the basement he frowned at the boxes they had collected down here already, not too many, but he knew he would have to clear them.

Placing Susan on the floor under the pipe that was set into the wall, he placed the rucksack down on the floor, unzipped it and removed a pair of handcuffs. Lifting her body into a seated position as best he could, he clasped one of the cuffs on her right wrist, lifting both hands together and looping the other cuff over the pipe before clasping the other end to her right wrist. As he let go of her body she slumped and a slight murmur escaped from her, she was still unconscious but wouldn't be for long.

He picked up the rucksack and removed his knife from it. Placing the rucksack over both shoulders he climbed back up the stairs, moving quietly and listening for any noise from the children he hoped were in their rooms. Standing at the bottom of the staircase, his heart was thumping and his adrenaline was racing, as he began to climb. Reaching the top he heard the noise of the TV in one of the rooms and children behind the door, watching cartoons on a Friday evening. Holding the knife in his right hand, he placed the left on the round knob and turned it. As the door opened and he stepped inside, he saw the three small children sitting watching YouTube videos.

The smallest girl, Sarah, was closest to him, she began to look over her shoulder with a smile assuming it was her mother she had seen in the corner of her eye, then seeing the man with the knife she screamed but Malcolm was swift, he grabbed the four-year-old with his left arm, placing his big hand over her mouth, and holding the knife to her throat. The other children, Alexandria and Simon, screamed and jumped away from Malcolm, climbing on top of their beds.

"Quiet or I'll kill her," he bellowed. With that, the door of the bedroom across the hall flew open and there stood a twelve-year-old boy, closely followed by his fourteen-year-old brother. They went white when they saw Malcolm holding their new stepsister in his arms, and a large knife pressed against her neck. The little girl was crying hard, her body shaking with fear. "Corey and Will, I presume? Don't do anything stupid boys," Malcolm's voice was sinister. "You do what you're told, and she'll be just fine. If not I'll kill her and then the both of you." The boys began to cry at the sight of the man with the knife and the mention of them being killed.

Malcolm looked briefly into the room at the two kids crying on the bed, and then back at the boys. "Carefully, and slowly, take them by the hand and start heading down to the basement." The boys didn't move initially, they were frozen in place until Malcolm barked at them, "Now!! Or she dies." Will, the older of the two boys moved first, slowly, towards the room and the doorway where the man was standing. He edged past Malcolm and went into the room.

"Simon, quickly, it's ok, go with Corey," he reached out his hand to his young stepbrother who grabbed it quickly and rushed in for a hug, "come on its ok, go with Corey." The little boy rushed out of the room and squeezed into his protector. "Come on Alex," he went over to her and picked her up, she wrapped her arms around him and shut her eyes.

"Downstairs," ordered Malcolm to the gang of kids, "straight into the basement." Their crying echoed around the hallway as they descended, Malcolm following closely behind. As Will and his brother reached the bottom of the stairs Malcolm was concerned about the boy's intentions, so he pressed the knife into the little girl's throat briefly making her scream. "Don't get any ideas, Will, she'll be dead, and you'll be next." Will turned around the bottom of the bannister and headed down the hall to the door at the top of the stairs that lead to the basement, closely followed by Corey.

As the group of children headed down to the basement, Malcolm heard the screams from them as they saw their mother, handcuffed with her arms above her head. As he entered the room, still holding his prisoner, they all screamed again, huddled into their mother who was just coming round from her experience with the tazer. Placing the little girl, Sarah, on the floor and allowing her to run over to her mother, he dropped the rucksack, still brandishing the blade in his hand. Kicking it over to Will. "Take out the handcuffs and restrain your siblings." Will didn't move initially, the skinny lad cast his eyes at the door. "Don't be stupid Will, this knife will land in your back before you get one step up those stairs." The boy, thinking better of it, reached for the bag, unzipped it and rummaged for a set of cuffs, tears streaming down his reddened cheeks. He took Sarah, the youngest girl over to the pipe where her step-mother was chained, the girl, four years old, was terrified. He lifted her arm and fumbled with the handcuff until he got it around one wrist, looping it over the pipe and fastening it to the other wrist.

Thursday, April 13th, 6am

When the alarm went off at six, Ash hit the snooze button and rolled over to spoon Lisa. She stirred and pulled him even closer. They lay there together until the phone rang out its second morning call, with Ash immediately going full stretch in the bed and letting out a long groan.

"Fuck it," he said as he got up from the bed, "sleep in babes, no need for you to get up this morning." She murmured a satisfied grunt of agreement. As he turned the shower on in the ensuite he used his phone to set the coffee machine downstairs, he loved the smell of coffee in the kitchen after a hot shower.

Once dressed he kissed Lisa on the cheek, and placed his hand on her stomach, "Love you both," he said.

"We love you too," she replied without opening her eyes.

In the kitchen the news was on the TV, Ash was catching up on the riot action throughout the night and the reports of the dead body of Mr. Kalarahi being found. He checked his phone, messages from Brad and Jim which he replied to and he sipped his coffee before heading to the car. On the drive into work, he felt his stomach rumble and pulled into an industrial estate to find his favourite snack van. Loading up with double bacon and another coffee he returned to his car and drove one-handed, biting into the roll as he did.

As he navigated the next couple of streets he took a sip of coffee, realising too late the lid wasn't secured and spilt it down his shirt. "Fuck," he shouted as he tried to simultaneously return the cup to the holder between the seats and pull the scalding wet cotton away from his skin. Managing to pull to the side of the road, he opened the door and climbed out of the car. Mumbling swear words under his breath he waited for the shirt to cool down. As he stood he looked up at the sky, taking deep breaths and cursing his stupidity in his own head.

Tucking his stained shirt back into his trousers, Ash glanced across the road. Something caught his eye through a chain mail gate. What appeared to be the roof of a white box van was just poking into view. Curiosity flowed through him as he closed the door to his car and walked across the street and up to the gate. Looking into the courtyard he could see a dozen shipping containers in almost a horseshoe shape, rusted in the most part, sitting behind a courtyard of rough stones. Behind one of the containers, he could see more clearly the roof of a panel van. He lifted the metal bar out of the hole in the ground, pushed the gate open and stepped inside, walking slowly forwards, down the slight slope that formed the entrance drive. He noticed only one other vehicle in the courtyard, an old-style Fiesta, sitting just off to the left.

Looking around, he continued on his way to the container in front of the van, stood for a second, and then walked the twenty feet along its edge. Reaching the rear roller door of the panel van, he unfastened the catch, and with both hands pushed it up. His eyes stood transfixed on the bloodstains inside the van and a surge of adrenalin pulsed through his body. He reached into his pocket for his phone and as he did he heard a footstep behind him. As he spun around he was hit hard in the chest, rocking him back against the floor of the van. He looked at Malcolm in front of him, Malcolm's arm was outstretched, and as he lowered it Ash slowly looked down at his chest.

The handle of the knife was visible, as Malcolm lunged forward again, covering Ash's mouth with his free hand and pulling the knife from Ash's rib cage, and plunging it over and over again into his stomach, ripping open his abdomen. Ash felt his attacker's strength, and his body had nothing to fight back with. He felt his knees buckle, he wanted to fall, but Malcolm held him up, looking directly into Ash's eyes, watching the life drain out of them. Ash thought about Lisa and his child as his mind went dark. Malcolm stood, holding Ash in place for a few more seconds, then scooped his legs, flipping Ash over and onto the bed of the van. He stood there for a moment, watching the legs and arms of his victim twitch, blood coughing from his mouth, gurgling, and pouring from his body from the multiple stab wounds. After a moment or two, the body rested, and the gurgles stopped. Malcolm reached up and pulled the roller door down.

Thursday, April 13th, 8.30am

Jim and Brad sat in Alison's office at 8.30am, sipping coffee and looking drained, even after a night's sleep. "Five major cities rioting after Harry's fuck you to them and Malcolm," declared Alison, "you have him in custody?"

"Yes Ma'am," replied Jim, "he'll get bail, but we could hold him for 48 hours."

Brad chimed in, "I say we let him out, see what happens to him." Not a popular suggestion out loud, although one they would all like to do, the looks from Jim and Alison made him regret saying it.

"The old man in the morgue yet," she asked.

"Yes Ma'am, dumped in the same fashion as Wendy, killed the same way too." Jim was searching for more to say. They were running empty in terms of leads. "We're doing everything we can."

"I don't doubt that, Jim," she leaned forward in her chair, resting her arms on the desk, "Unless you get lucky, this is going right to Sunday night." She stood up from her desk, straightening her shirt, "I have to report to the media, keep me posted gents." With that, she walked out of the office leaving Jim and Brad sitting quietly.

After a couple of moments, Jim piped up, "Have we got anything new?" He looked across at Brad.

"Nope." Brad cradled his cup in the palm of his hand. "We are goosed. Any forensics we are getting is not helping because Malcolm is not hiding his DNA. Garden to garden has been widened and is still coming up empty."

"He's holed up somewhere, with everything he needs. He moves to post videos, drop off bodies," Jim downed the last of his now lukewarm coffee "he has everything he needs to finish the week. What happens then?" He had initially asked it as a rhetorical question, as he rose from his seat.

"He'll either go out in a blaze of glory or disappear," Brad got to his feet, looking directly at Jim as he said it.

"Both of which are scary as fuck!" Jim left the room first, glancing down at his watch as he stepped into the corridor. "Ash is taking his time."

"He'll be in Ops, boss." Brad's phone buzzed in his pocket. He removed it and read the notification allowed. "Video posted ... this guy loves himself"

Entering the Ops room Jim nodded at a detective hovering over the play button on the screen. The now familiar style in which Malcolm made his videos began to play.

"Ladies and Gentleman of Great Britain, what a spectacle you all put on last night. Firstly, congratulations to Harry Kalarahi, you showed me didn't you, but I was not surprised at all, and to be honest, how many of you out there are thinking that at least poor Mr. Kalarahi is at peace now. Well, I hope that's enough to keep you safe Harry, I am pretty sure there are some meatheads out there looking for a prize.

"As for the riots, wow, you all know how to vent your anger, don't you. I'm not sure whether that anger is aimed at me, or the vulgar acts of immorality I am unmasking this week. Nonetheless, I am pleased you are all showing your true passion.

"Well, what about tonight's choice. Claire Papadopoulos and her boyfriend Gregory. Gregory is safely with me, a genuinely nice guy, and the kind of guy that would make a mother in law happy. Claire on the other hand, well she's just trouble. She's currently sleeping with her boyfriend's boss, and has slept with many bosses, many random strangers, and is a frequent visitor of the cubicles in many London pubs. Gregory is blind to these acts, and one gets the feeling he was about to propose. So, Claire, what's it to be?"

With that, the video ended. "Where is she?" Jim asked Brad.

"We'll bring her in, boss." Brad turned to a colleague and began making instructions. He was interrupted by Jim.

"And where is Ash?" He looked around the room, taking his phone from his pocket. Dialling his number it went straight to "The number you are dialling cannot be contacted" and he hung up. "Has anyone seen Chilton?" The faces of the other detectives and constables looked blank. He walked over to his desk as Brad followed.

Brad tried dialling from his phone, receiving the same message as Jim "Not connecting, boss, want me to try Lisa?"

He shook his head, looking at his watch, "9.15, give it a while, maybe they're having a domestic."

A detective approached Jim and Brad. "Claire Papadopoulos had gone to her mother's for the last couple of nights," he stated, "we have a car bringing her in."

June, 2015

Claire stood at the bar, holding her ten-pound note out to catch Wesley, the barman's, attention. He looked over at her, "Same again?" and she nodded, giving him her usual cheeky smile.

"You're the best Wesley," she shouted. The pub was busy as usual for a Saturday, the landlord had a band over in the corner, typical cheesy music but they got the crowd going. As she leaned on the bar, glancing back at her friends in the booth in the corner, she turned back to see if Wesley was pouring her drink yet as a guy approached and leaned next to her.

"Can I buy you one?" he asked, looking at Claire. She gave him a once over, looking him up and down. Reasonably dressed, shirt, jeans, well-groomed, and in his early thirties. She looked briefly back at the girls in the booth, all having fun and not paying attention to her.

"Sure," she smiled, "Wesley is just pouring it." The barman placed her drink on the bar and her new friend handed over a note, as Claire placed her money back in her clutch. "I'm Claire."

"Dave," he offered, "so, you meeting anyone?"

"I just have," she replied, she had never had much of an issue with confidence. She was tall, blonde, and had a good figure that she looked after. She also dressed to attract, wearing short skirts, tight tops, she always knew what she was doing. Her boyfriend was out with his mates, and she had very little concept of loyalty. She liked sex, and she knew how to get it.

The two stood flirting for a few minutes, but Claire didn't have all night. "Listen, Dave," she said as she leaned a little closer, stroking her fingertips up his arm, "I'm not here to spend all night chatting to you so if you wanna fuck follow me." Dave smiled, placing his drink on the bar. She took him by the hand and led him through the busy bar to the toilets, winking at one of her friends as she did. As she entered the toilets she checked to see they were empty, pulling Dave inside and pushing him into one of the cubicles, locking it behind them.

In the cramped space, she began kissing him, his hands exploring her body, as she fumbled at his belt buckle, managing to release it. She moved her hands to her skirt, pulling it up, as he pushed down his jeans and shorts. She bent over, hand on the cistern as he fucked her from behind. The sex didn't last long before he came inside her. The moment he had, he withdrew and she grabbed some toilet roll from the dispenser, cleaning herself up. "Good job, Dave," she said, kissing him, "nice cock too." He pulled his jeans up, before leaving the cubicle, bumping into a couple of women who were entering as he was leaving, giving him grief as he did.

Claire stood in the cubicle, it had a been a quick fuck, but a good one and her legs were shaking. She wiped herself clean and pulled up her knickers. As she adjusted her skirt she stepped out into the bathroom approaching the sinks and mirrors where the other two women were stood adjusting their makeup. Ignoring them as she checked herself in the mirror, she left the toilets.

Returning to the bar area, she walked to the booth with her friends, instantly getting attention from the girls who wanted all the details. On a table a few feet away sat Malcolm, drinking a pint of beer. He was watching as the blonde woman went into the toilets with the guy, and then returned fifteen minutes later. He could hear her telling the story to her girlfriends, with one of them asking about someone called Gregory, and Claire's response being "what he doesn't know won't hurt him."

Thursday, April 13th, 11am

At just after 11, Jim and Brad entered the family room where Claire was sitting with her Mum on the cheap Ikea couch. "Miss Papadopoulos," Jim extended a hand to Claire which she shook, "Mrs. Papadopoulos?" He asked with an inflection towards the older woman.

"What are you people doing here?" blurted out the mother, disregarding the offer of the handshake.

"Ma'am, this is a unique situation." Jim was cut off abruptly. "I don't care what kind of situation this is, my daughter is not going anywhere tonight," she placed an arm around her. "My daughter's name has been plastered all over the internet, she's been humiliated, and you fools seem unable to solve this case."

Jim leaned back in his chair, glanced over at Brad who was still stood by the door, and then back at Claire. "Claire, I would like you to stay here for the day if that's ok, you'll be close at hand if we have any leads."

"I can't do it," she whimpered, "I do love him, but I …" Her mother pulled her in close.

"Detective," Her voice had mellowed, "Please don't make my daughter go through this, go and find him." Jim rose from his seat and Brad pulled open the door.

"It's all we are trying to do Ma'am, that I can promise." He left the room with Brad in tow. "Where the fuck is Ash?" He was getting worried. The young detective had never been late a day in his life, it wasn't his style. "Call Lisa, but don't worry her."

"She's a pregnant woman dating a Detective boss," retorted Brad, "a Detective involved in this crazy case, I think it would be easier catching Malcolm than not worrying her." Jim wasn't in the mood for jokes, Brad quickly regretted his smart mouth and dialled Lisa from his mobile.

After a couple of rings, it answered, "Hey Brad," she was chirpy, "what's up old-timer?"

"Hi Lisa, Ash left his phone on his desk," he was sincere with his lie, "if he pops in tell him to call me will ya."

"Sure thing," she hesitated, "everything ok? Did you catch him yet?"

"No Hun, not yet. How's my little bump?" He glanced at Jim as they walked the corridor, shaking his head as he spoke.

"Oh ya know, moving the furniture around," she laughed.

"Well ya know she's gonna have my eyes," he smiled down the phone, "just don't tell Ash."

"It's our little secret Hun, I promise," with that they both hung up. Brad slid his phone into his pocket.

"Where the fuck is he?" Jim snapped as they entered the Ops room and walked over to his desk. Jim was irritable, dozens of men and women on the case and they were getting nowhere, and now one of his best didn't show up for work. He picked up a file on his desk and feigned opening it, before slamming it now on the desk, "FUCK FUCK FUCK," he hollered. The remaining officers in the room stopped and stared at Jim.

"Jim," said Brad sternly, keeping his voice low, "For fuck's sake now is not the time, and this is not the place." He pulled up a chair and sat opposite him. Jim knew, he was well versed in keeping his cool, but he knew this was one awful situation to be in. Three days into Malcolm's game and they were no closer to catching him. Their colleagues had continued working, tracking every lead no matter how loose.

Leaning forward in the chair, Jim stared at Brad, "Where the fuck is Ash, I got a bad feeling Brad."

Friday, April 7th, 5pm

In the basement the children sat crying, huddling in to each other as best they could, their arms aching from the cuffs that held them captive. Susan has come round following her shock, initially screaming and crying, but after a while, she calmed enough to try and comfort her children. As she sat on the stone floor she had tried to ask Malcolm what he was doing and why they were chained up, but he had ignored every word she said, carefully taking the boxes up the stairs one by one, leaving nothing but the captive family in the basement. After several attempts she chose to talk to her children instead, trying to get them to stop crying, trying her best to comfort them and tell them it was going to be ok.

Sitting on a wooden stool in the corner, Malcolm did not flinch. He sat perfectly still, biding his time and ignoring the woman who was begging to have her children freed. After some time, Malcolm looked down at his watch. He rose to his feet and walked over to the girl he had held before, Sarah, reaching his hand into his pocket and taking out a key.

"Don't you fucking touch her!" screamed her mother, who began lashing out with her legs as Malcolm carefully unlocked the cuffs. The girl began to scream, but as Malcolm adjusted her in his arms he managed to get his big hands around her mouth again, and quickly the little girl was silenced. "Put her fucking down, put her fucking down" the woman was incensed, seeing her step-daughter manhandled by this brutish stranger, terrified beyond belief. The little girl had tears running down her face as Malcolm reached back into his rucksack that was lying on the floor and removed the twelve-inch blade. Susan managed to get to her feet, pulling her wrists against the cuffs, trying with all her might to get to Sarah and keep her safe.

"SIT DOWN!" bellowed Malcolm, raising the knife to the girl's belly. His eyes pierced deep into Susan and she silenced herself immediately. Malcolm did not flinch, staring at the woman whose legs were wobbling beneath her.

"Ok …. Ok," Susan began to bend her knees, "just don't hurt her, please, don't hurt her." With that she sat back down on the floor, her breath rapid and her eyes red. The children were all crying, still trying to gain as much comfort as possible, huddling their bodies close to each other.

"I'm going up to wait for your fella," said Malcolm calmly, "if I hear any screams this little one is dead." With that Malcolm stepped out of the room and climbed the stairs to the hallway above. He walked into the front room, standing in the centre, with the little girl clasped firmly in his grasp and stood looking out of the bay window.

After fifteen minutes, Darren parked his car squarely in front of the terraced house, right in front of the spot where Malcolm had parked his own. Malcolm watched as he saw Darren sitting in the car for a few moments, dusk was drawing in, the inside of the car illuminated by his mobile phone. After a few seconds, the driver door opened and Darren stepped out, grabbing a shopping bag from the passenger seat as he did. As he rounded the car he clicked the fob, illuminating the hazard lights. Darren headed for the stairs, with Malcolm moving back into the hallway. The noise of keys jangling just outside the door made Malcolm tense up, holding the blade to the little girl's throat. As the door opened, Darren was looking down at the floor, catching the door with his right hand and pushing it shut. The hallway returned to shadow, "Hey babes …" he cut off his usual welcome as he saw the silhouette of the man in front of him, "What the fuck!" He reached out his arm and instinctively flicked on the light switch. His eyes could barely comprehend what was in front of him, the sight of his youngest daughter's eyes staring at him, a huge hand of the man holding her clasped around her mouth, and knife at her throat. He felt his knees shake and he reached out for the hallway wall to steady himself, "Whatever it is, don't hurt her," his trembling voice managed.

"Darren, welcome home," Malcolm smiled from behind the little girl. "We have a lot to discuss."

1993

Isabella sat on the metal stairs crying as a cold breeze from the door above chilled her back. Sitting alone, her sobs fell on silent walls and her tears rolled down her cheeks with no one to dab them dry. After her ordeal with Jimboy and his friends, she had run to find her brother, searched for hours and eventually found herself at the top of the stairwell, sitting freezing and shivering, trying to find solace in the portion of now cold chips she held in her hands.

Her brother was the only family she had now. Her mother, still at home, was hardly a mother. Malcolm had raised her since she was about four years old, even though only a couple of years older himself. Occasionally the social services had placed them in foster care, but eventually, her mother had always got them back. Even at thirteen, Isabella knew the only reason her mother wanted them was for the money, her kids were an income for her, a way to get the funds for another bottle of vodka. If it wasn't for her brother she wouldn't eat, have any clean clothes and certainly wouldn't be at school. Life was hard, but he made it so much better.

As she dragged the back of her hand across her cheek, smearing tears down the back of her wrist, she thought about the punch she had received from one of the girls in Jimboy's group. She had been knocked to the ground and had curled up in a ball. Fighting three girls while four boys chanted on was not an option for her. She hadn't been punched before, but the ritual tormenting had happened on a frequent basis for the past year. When Isabella had started at the high school she had kept her head down, following her brothers lead as he had been there for a couple of years, giving her good advice to be able to survive. Neither of them had much and were both constantly teased for not having the popular Nike or Reebok trainers, or for having a school shirt that wasn't properly clean, or even for not having lunch with them or money to buy it. Jimboy had heard that their mother was an alcoholic after hearing teachers discussing it. The bully in him did the rest, seeking out opportunities to make both Malcolm and Isabella suffer.

Malcolm and he were the same age, and on several occasions they had come to blows, the larger Jimboy, supported by his pals, had always gotten the better of the smaller boy, the odds never being even, with Malcolm receiving his unfair share of black eyes and fat lips. The girls that jeered and crowed at while Jimboy set about Malcolm, then became fascinated with Isabella, beginning their own undeserved vendetta against her. Each time they isolated her, their behaviour had worsened, starting with name-calling, pushing, spitting, and eventually escalating to the ordeal Isabella had suffered earlier in the day.

The young girl had been walking home from school, alone as she had not been able to find Malcolm at the gates. She could hear the girls with Jimboy and the lads following her about twenty feet behind, and she was panicking, trying not to show it but she could sense trouble. The group was actively talking about her, and her mother, making crude suggestions about what she did to earn money to drink all of that vodka. Ahead of her was the underpass she needed to walk through to get home, her heart was beating out of her chest as she approached it. From where she was she could see it was clear all the way through, but she was really worried about the group behind her.

As she approached the entrance to the tunnel she began to pick up her pace.

"Ha! The little cunts scared," shouted Nicola, one of the girls, and at that Isabella tried to run, not realising the group had caught up with her. As she tried to get up to full speed she could hear the echoing of their feet and laughter right behind her. She was frightened, but felt a moment of bravery, stopping suddenly and turning to face them. She was about to shout at them, the scenario in her head suggested if she spun around and shouted at them they would stop. Instead, Nicola ran straight into her, dipping her shoulder and knocking her to the ground. She hit the concrete hard, palms first, scuffing them but managing to keep her head from connecting with the hard surface.

"What's your fucking problem," she screamed at Isabella, leaning right over her, inches from her face. The knockdown had been swift, and between the fright and the scuffed palms, Isabella burst into tears, "you nearly knocked me over you stupid cunt!" Nicola glared right into Isabella's face, with Jimboy and her friends taunting her, surrounding her as she lay on the ground. The poor girl couldn't speak, as her attacker raised a fist, striking her hard on the side of the eye, splitting the skin instantly.

At that moment, a man walking his dog entered the alleyway from the same direction the gang had come from, Jimboy spotted him. "Let's go," he ordered his little group, and they bolted in the opposite direction, laughing as they went. Isabella began to pick herself up as the man stood at the other end with his dog, his head was bowed down and he had slowed his pace. Her legs were trembling following her attack, but she managed to walk and headed out of the tunnel, in the direction of her home.

Blood trickled down the side of her face as she pulled down on the handle of her front door and stepped inside, dropping her schoolbag on top of the mountain of letters just inside the entrance. She walked along the hallway and into the front room, looking at the snoring, fat excuse of a mother laying on the couch. The ashtray on the coffee table was full, the bottle next to it lay on its side, drained as usual. She looked down at her mother's hand, a cigarette was burning away between her yellow fingers. Although the house was not much to look at, it was the only place she had a bed and she didn't want it burnt to the ground, so she leant down taking the cigarette carefully and stubbing it out on the pile of butts.

Walking upstairs she had hoped to see Malcolm in his room, but it was empty. Turning to walk into her room she lifted the lid on the keepsake box she kept on her bedside table. Inside was a pound coin and a note from Malcolm, "For chips". He was out, but he always made sure there was something for her to eat, even if it meant walking to the chippy. She didn't really fancy going back out again, but she was starving. Unrolling some tissue from a toilet roll on the cabinet she looked in the mirror, dabbing the cut on her eyebrow. It didn't look too bad but she winced as she touched it. Holding the tissue in place she popped the coin into her pocket and headed back out of the house.

The chip bag was warm in her hands, the cut above her eye had stopped bleeding and she had decided to go and sit on the stairs at the top of the tower, hoping that Malcolm would stop there as he often did. So many times they had hung out at the top of the tower, sometimes laying on a blanket outside on the fibreglass roof looking up at the sky, or if it was raining, inside on the metal stairs talking, just chatting about anything that would make them smile. As she ate her chips in peace, she heard footsteps on the concrete stairs below, and after a few seconds, the door at the bottom of the stairs opened.

She had hoped it was Malcolm, but instead, a lad called Darren stood at the foot of the stairs. She knew him from school, the same year as her brother, but she had not had many dealings with him. The boy, stocky, crew-cut hair, stood and looked up at her.

"Your Malcolm's sister right?"

"Uh-huh," she didn't say anything, but took another chip from the paper and slowly placed it in her mouth.

Darren looked up at her, cocking his head as he spotted the cut above her eye, "Who did that?"

She stared down at him, dropping her gaze when she replied, "No one, obviously." Snitches get stitches, she might not have liked her attackers but no one on these estates grassed.

The lad took a step up. "You gonna give me some of those chips?" Isabella looked at him, the fear was back, and she did not like this at all.

"Here you can have them," she said as she got to her feet, heading down towards the boy, offering the chip papers, "I have to get home anyways." She was level with Darren, about to walk past, when he stepped in front of her.

"Nah nah, you're gonna keep me company while I eat them," he stared directly at her, placing his arm across her path and putting his palm against the concrete wall, stopping her from getting past.

Isabella paused for a brief second and then tried to push past. He was strong and didn't budge, she looked into his eyes, almost sensing his intentions. He slammed the palm of his hand down onto the chip papers she was still holding, scattering them all over the bottom of the stairs. Isabella let out a yelp, and instantly tried to push past him, "No you fucking don't you little cunt," he said as his big hands grabbed her, "I've heard about you, turning tricks for your old lady." He had both hands grabbing her arms, and he spun her around quickly, pushing her down on the stairs. Isabella's cheekbone struck the edge of a step, sending a sharp white pain through her eyes. Darren had the weight of his body pressed against her, she screamed as Darren grabbed the waistband of her leggings, pulling them down with two distinctive tugs. She was unable to move beneath him, as he pulled his hard cock from his tracksuit bottoms, forcing himself inside of her. He thrust into her, over and over, before finishing and standing up.

He looked at her, laying sobbing on the stairs, as she was trying to pull her leggings back up, he laughed at her. He put his hand in his pocket and pulled out some change, throwing it at her, "There, I paid for it!" With that he disappeared down the stairwell, laughing as he went, with the sound echoing all the way.

She reached her hand up, taking hold of the rail, easing herself off the ground, managing eventually to get to both feet. Pulling her leggings up she felt the wetness between her legs making her physically shake, staggering to the top of the tower block stairwell she began to descend carefully. The tears did not subside, she climbed down the twenty stories slowly with them rolling down her cheeks. It took her more than an hour to reach the bottom. She needed to find Malcolm, desperately, he would know what to do.

As she stepped out into the courtyard of the tower block she managed to walk straight and headed for home.

As she made it across the courtyard she saw a police car heading towards her, driving along the road. She thought about waving it down, but as it passed she saw her brother Malcolm in the back seat, he saw her at the last second, spinning his head in her direction but the car continued its journey. She collapsed to her knees in the street, head bowed down to the ground as she wailed. After a few moments, she lifted her head and turned around, ahead of her was the top of the tower block where she had just been raped.

Friday, April 7th, 9pm

Darren's eyes opened, with an instantaneous pain surging between his temples. Malcolm had hit Darren with the tazer as he approached him in the entrance hallway. After carrying the girl downstairs and returning her to her handcuffs, he took the bottle of chloroform and made sure the man was unconscious, before dragging his body down the stairs and using another pair of cuffs to restrain him, gagging his mouth with the silver gaffer tape. Malcolm sat opposite him on his stool, looking directly at him as he came round, with a grin on his face. Glancing to his side he saw his family, his wife, and their children, it took a fraction of a second for him to realise that he and they were restrained, causing him to attempt to scream, and a further realisation that his mouth was obstructed by tape, resulting in distorted grunting sound, forcing his eyes to bulge with panic.

"Hello there, Darren, it's been a long time," Malcolm sat very still. Darren's panicked eyes were blemished with an air of confusion, this man in front of him was not familiar and yet seemed to know him. His wife sat on the floor next to him, looked at Darren with a similar confused expression, the children whimpering. Malcolm leaned forward slightly, his next word spoken with a whisper, "Isabella." Darren's eyes changed again, and suddenly fear filled them.

Malcolm shifted his gaze to Susan, "Hi Susan, you've been wondering why I am here, why you and your beloved children are in this current predicament, well your husband here is the reason. You see, some years ago I had a sister, Isabella, and when she was just thirteen, your husband raped her, and she took her own life because of him." Susan was crying behind her gag, her head shaking from side to side, her mouth mumbling the word "no" over and over again with the words barely audible. Malcolm stood up and walked over towards the youngest girl, reaching his hand into his pocket and removing the key before continuing, "Isabella was my life, but to my shame, I was not there for her when she needed me most. That is my burden to bare." He leant down and unlocked the girl's handcuffs, causing a frenzy of movement from Susan and Darren, trying hard to pull their wrists from their restraints, kicking their legs out fruitlessly in Malcolm's direction. Malcolm dragged the girl by the wrist towards the gurney. "For years I now I have imagined what Darren would do if his loved ones were taken from him," lifting the little girl onto the gurney, fixing her restraints, using his strength to hold her in place. "You see, Darren has gone on to have a pretty good life, he's been married, had kids, divorced, and even remarried, and he has not paid for his crime." Finally, with the girl's restraints in place, he walked over to his rucksack sitting by the stool, bending down and sliding his hand inside, taking hold of his knife and removing it. The screams and thrashing got louder from Susan and Darren, the crying from the children became shrill. As he walked back towards the girl on the gurney he continued, "I have suffered a lifetime of loss because of you Darren, but fortunately for you, you won't suffer for long," he was stood with the gurney between himself and the family, "you see, I'm going to kill you last." With that, he placed his left hand on the girl's forehead, and with his right, he placed the knife on the far side of her jugular. Digging the point of the knife into her throat he slowly pulled the blade towards him, splitting the skin and severing the artery, blood spurting instantly into the air, covering Malcolm's white t-shirt, and spraying onto the floor. He stood very still, staring directly at Darren as the twitching body of his youngest daughter began to lose its life, the legs settling, the blood slowing as her heart stopped. He placed the knife down at the foot of the gurney.

Darren was screaming, pulling himself against pipe he was cuffed to, his wife had closed her eyes and was motionless. Slowly Malcolm removed the little girls' restraints, picked up her lifeless body, soaked in blood, and carried her upstairs to the dining room. On the table he had rolled out a large sheet of plastic, placing her carefully down and folding over the sheets. Once she was wrapped, he lifted the body once more and placed her down on the floor in the corner before returning downstairs.

"Now," Malcolm continued with his little speech, "the problem with grief, is sometimes it's very hard to get over. This particular type of grief was difficult for me, and whereas some people would have a sense of justification if the perpetrator of such a crime was held accountable..." He paused and he walked towards the youngest of the boys, sending the family into a panic again, muffled screams and the sound of cuffs rattling against the pipes filled the room. "But in your case Darren, the police questioned you, but never charged you." He unlocked the little boys' cuffs, scooping him up in his arms. The five-year-old thrashed out but Malcolm's size meant that he was easily able to control him. "Which was interesting because everyone on the estate knew you had raped my little sister." He was strapping the boy to the table, the little girl's blood on the gurney and Malcolm's hands marking her brother's t-shirt. Restraining the boy in the headrest, Malcolm looked into the eyes of the terrified boy, before looking directly at Darren. "You must have been telling quite the tales, but no one would grass on you, even with the DNA evidence there was not enough to charge you with rape, I believe you told them it was consensual, and as you were only 15 yourself there was nothing the police could do." He picked up the knife. "My sister was innocent, and you killed her." He dug the knife into Simon's throat, opening it up with a fountain of blood escaping. The family were all screaming, legs flailing, wrists beginning to bleed as they tried in vain to free themselves. When the body gave up the fight for life, Malcolm lay the knife at the foot of the gurney again and began unfastening the straps. Carrying the body upstairs, he wrapped it in plastic and lay him next to his sister, before returning to the basement.

Susan was tiring, the experience of watching two children being killed had numbed her brain. The realisation of the situation, and what was happening was too much for her to take, and she passed out. Malcolm looked at the family, scanning the three remaining children, the wife, and finally looking back at Darren. "So, you raped my sister, my beautiful Isabella," moving to Darren's eldest child, Alexandria, the little one curled up in a ball, arms above her head held firm by her cuffs. "And you laughed about it with your mates." He freed the girl's wrists, grabbing onto her tightly, dragging her across the smooth concrete floor towards the gurney. "You then became an adult, found love and got married." The girl was lifted onto the black mattress which was now soaked with blood and Malcolm set to work on his restraints, placing one hand firmly on the girl's chest to hold her in place. "You had these beautiful kids, but still couldn't be a decent human being." Looking at Darren, the girl now unable to move, Malcolm reached for his blade. "You cheated on their mother, causing them heartache they did not deserve." He slit Alexandria's throat, watching his father scream, hanging his head low, laying his head as close to the ground as his restrained arms would allow him.

With the girl now wrapped in plastic upstairs next to her siblings, Malcolm stood in front of Susan. "Susan, wake up, Susan." Malcolm kicked her ankles, causing her head to lift. "You cheated on your husband Susan, with a rapist." Looking at her two sons, he added, "You turned their world upside down." She stared into Malcolm's eyes, begging and pleading without being able to say a word. Malcolm looked back at Darren. "I'm going to put the boys out of their misery now, Darren, and it's all your fault." With a ferocious and fast attack he stepped towards the boys, stabbing the youngest of them in the chest, withdrawing the blade and plunging it into his brother's neck. Malcolm was fast, not enough time for the boys to comprehend what was happening, their mother thrashed her body in a vain attempt to defend them. Blood poured and spat onto their clothes, their bodies twitched. Malcolm went into a frenzy, stabbing and slashing at the bodies, over and over, as Susan and Darren screamed through the gaffer tape. Malcolm stopped his attack and a few moments passed before the movement ceased from the bodies of Corey and Will, their mother sat staring at them, no life in her eyes, barely able to catch her breath. Malcolm controlled his breathing, looking over at Darren, "I didn't do it." He placed his knife on the ledge and began the process of taking the bodies upstairs.

"Now," he said to Darren, once he had returned from the dining room, "your wife is going to die, that much I think you have worked out." Susan didn't flinch, she had all but given up after watching the five children she loved be brutally murdered by this maniac. "However, I don't think it should be that simple, you see Isabella suffered before she died." He walked over to his rucksack, removing the tazer. "I have one final surprise for you." He leant down and tazered Darren in the leg, causing him to convulse and pass out.

When Darren came round, he took a few moments to focus his eyes. His wife was no longer sitting next to him. He looked up towards the gurney. Malcolm had his wife bent over the width of the gurney, from where Darren sat on the floor he could stare straight into Susan's eyes, she was awake, looking straight at her husband. His tormentor stood behind his wife. "Welcome back, I'll kill you after this." He had handcuffed Susan to the framework of the gurney and had removed her trousers and underwear. "You see, you weren't just the cause of Isabella's death, you raped her, and you enjoyed it. Well, I'm not going to enjoy this, but an eye for an eye." He unbuckled his belt, removing his cock from his jeans, placing his bloodied hands on her back, he parted her legs with his and raped her. Fucking her hard, over and over as she screamed and Darren cried. Malcolm had no intention of satisfying himself, and after a minute withdrew his cock. Buckling himself up, he stared directly at Darren, looking to his side he picked up the knife, pulling her hair back and raising her chin, he slit her throat, spraying blood over the concrete floor.

As her body slumped and her legs buckled, he walked towards Darren. Malcolm's rage was building, the knife still in his hand as he stood towering over the man who had raped his sister all those years ago. His family now all dead, Darren stared at the lifeless body of his dead wife. A raging scream left Malcolm's mouth as he plunged the knife into Darren's abdomen, pulling it clear and then began ferociously slashing away at him. He didn't stop until the muscles in his body were exhausted until he physically couldn't plunge the blade into the body anymore.

Thursday, April 12th, 8pm

"Alison, he hasn't been heard from, not since 7 this morning," Jim and Brad were sitting opposite her again. "Brad's phoned his girlfriend twice, she's worried and rightly so, I don't think we can placate her much longer."

Alison leaned back in her chair, "Jesus, Jim, you think Malcolm has him?" She let out a sigh.

"Ash has a keen eye, Ma'am," Brad offered, "I can only think he may have seen something, followed a lead and got himself into trouble. We have every squad car in London scanning for his plate."

"We've got an hour until Claire needs to be at Trafalgar," Jim stood up, "I'm gonna go get her, and her mum if she's still here. I'm pretty confident poor Gregory will turn up not breathing tonight, but we might be surprised." As he walked to the door, he turned back, "Extra riot police, push the cordons back …"

"It's done, Jim," snapped Alison, the tension in the room was not personal, but Brad eased himself out of the door without antagonising the situation, followed by Jim. As the two men walked down to the waiting room not much was said. They were both tired, and whereas a couple of nights, ago they held out hope for a good result, they were now almost resigned to accepting there would be a further corpse in the morgue tonight.

Opening the door of the waiting room, both of them stopped when they saw it was empty. "Get her on the phone," Jim said as he turned out of the room. A female officer was walking towards him, "Where is she?"

"They were in there twenty minutes ago Guv," she looked startled.

"No answer," Brad offered, placing his phone in his pocket.

The desk sergeant came running through the door at the end of the corridor. "Guv, she left five minutes ago," the heavyset man was out of breath, presumably from his dash up the stairs, "her mother told me to back off when I tried to stop them."

"Jeez, what else is going to fuck this day up," shouted Jim, raising his hands to his head. He turned to Brad, "ideas?"

"Jim, I can't blame her," he placed his hands on his hips, "she told us clearly she wasn't going to do it, what's the difference if she's there or not." He looked at the two other officers in the corridor, "thanks guys, carry on." The portly desk sergeant headed back out the corridor, and the female officer walked past them in the opposite direction. "Jim, I say we go down to the chair and see what happens, this whole goddam week has been out of our control, mate. I say we ride it out and then try and find Ash."

"Fuck 'em," said Jim, he checked both directions in the corridor seeing that it was still clear, "there are four scared people trapped somewhere, and their own dam families don't want to save them, what bloody chance have we got. And then we have our friend missing." He paused, looking at the ground, "Ash has to be number one. We need to find him alive." Pulling his car keys from his pocket, "Let's go see what happens at the Square, and then head to Ash's apartment. We need to be upfront and honest with Lisa."

They arrived at the chair with fifteen minutes to go. The crowds were huge but MacHray had ensured the cordons were much further back and there were visibly more armed officers, including a good dozen on horseback. The noise was deafening, helicopters overhead, blue lights flashing as far as the eye could see. Jim looked over to the chair, a dozen armed officers stood in a horseshoe shape, each of them with their back to the chair about twenty feet away from it. He cast his eyes to the rooftops, spotting snipers training their guns onto the square. They stood and watched the scene before them, occasionally chatting to officers and fellow detectives, passing the time until they heard that first chime. As it rang across the city the crowds roared, louder than any football match either of them had been at. The riot officers seemed unthreatened this evening, but the crowd was vocalising their anger. Jim was unsure if it was at the police, at Malcolm, or at the absent Claire Papadopoulos, most likely all three. He looked at Brad and nodded, very soon Gregory would be dead, and there was nothing they could do about it.

Heading off in the car, they took the thirty-minute drive to Ash's apartment. Various calls made to the morgue, the control office and little talking between the two of them. Parking outside the block of apartments neither man really wanted to get out of the car. Jim levering the handle first and climbing out. Walking up the front steps they pressed the buzzer and waited for the intercom. "Hello," the crackle of Lisa's voice broke the beep.

"It's Jim," with that they heard a brief sob and the door buzzed and clicked. Jim pushed it open and they took the lift to her floor. The door was ajar so they entered, "Lisa?" Jim called.

"In here Jim," they followed the low voice to the lounge, as they entered she asked, "Is he dead?"

"No," offered Jim, "but he is missing." Lisa was sitting hunched forward on the footstool, Jim took to the armchair and Brad sat on the couch. Her eyes were damp, she had been crying since she phoned Brad at 7 and learned that Ash had still not turned up.

"My Mum's coming down from Birmingham, she'll be here soon."

"I am so sorry Lisa," Brad said, "we're not going to stop until we find him."

Lisa looked up, placing her hands over her bump. "Just like the guys Malcolm has?" she asked. Brad, sat a little more upright at that remark. Instantly she regretted saying it, Brad was a particularly close friend and she knew they both cared deeply and were honest about trying to find him. "I'm sorry Brad … I'm a mess," she sobbed.

"Never apologise to me sweet girl," Brad said softly, "This has been a fucked up week until this morning, and now it's unbearable. If there is anything you can tell us, did he say anything before he left about stopping off somewhere?"

"Not a thing, he gave me and bump a kiss and went off with a smile." She paused, her eyes were recalling the last moments she saw Ash this morning, "he was fucking happy, he was sure he was going to solve this case. He wanted to make you guys happy."

The conversation was interrupted by another buzz at the door. "That's my Mum, guys," she said as she wiped a tear, and got up to walk towards the intercom. "Shit, I'm so sorry, I didn't offer you a cuppa"

"It's me darling" They heard her mum say.

"No, no, Lisa, please we'll let you be with your Mum," said Jim. "Keep your phone close and call us if you hear anything or need anything." He gave her a quick hug and opened the front door to the apartment.

Brad leaned in and used his index finger to wipe a tear away, "We'll fix this sweet girl," and he embraced her for a couple of seconds, releasing his big arms from round her he placed his hand on her belly. "Keep this one safe for when Ash gets home." With that, the two men left the apartment.

Thursday, April 12th, 11pm

Brad dropped Jim back at the Yard for his car, before heading off home. The drive back had been a quiet one, little conversation between the two of them was needed, and the chaos of the week almost demanded a little quiet thinking time. Brad had told Jim to get home, even suggesting he drop him off and pick him up in the morning to ensure he got some sleep. Jim had rebuffed the offer, deciding instead to drive and turn the volume up to maximum.

The roads were empty as Jim drove with American anthems blasting out. After a while, he couldn't help himself and he tuned into the radio, catching the headlines of the news. Riots were underway in various parts of London and other cities, but from the report, Trafalgar Square was quiet, more than likely due to the enforcement of additional riot officers and a stronger understanding that the public was on edge. Certain sections of London barley needed a spark to take to the streets, and this week, Malcolm's game, created an inferno. The crowds were angry at the police for their incompetence, regardless of the unique situation and the impossible task of finding this lunatic. They were angry at Malcolm for the killing of innocent people, and they were angry at the people tasked with sitting in that chair. Jim knew all this, but also knew that almost everyone had skeletons, including himself.

As he opened his front door he tossed the keys in the basket on the sideboard. Kicking his shoes off, he entered the front room, lifting a crystal tumbler from the drinks cabinet, and the bottle of Famous Grouse. Pouring himself a deep measure he reclined in his armchair. Sitting in the relative darkness of the front room he thought about the events of the week. George Russ the wife-beater, now sitting home alone planning a funeral for his wife. The young lad Chris Johnston, his future uncertain as his mother made the ultimate sacrifice to save his life. Harry Singh, the complete opposite parent/child relationship, no love, no guilt, no remorse for the loss of his father. And now somewhere, they would find the next victim, the innocent Gregory, who's seemingly only fault was loving a gorgeous blonde who liked to play with men for her own benefit.

Three more nights of this shit he thought to himself. Malcolm had orchestrated a very good game for himself, where the police had their hands tied, and he had managed to get the public involved in a way that there was no hiding from. He was exhausted, sipping the last of the whiskey in his glass he contemplated another one as his eyes began to close. He slept there till he woke at six.

Thursday, April 12th 9.10pm

With the low glow of the camping light in the corner of the container the muffled sobs of his prisoners were weak. He had just switched off the iPad which had been showing the news coverage of the empty chair, and then shots of the riots throughout the city. In the gloom he could see Gregory's eyes wide, petrified as he lifted the carving knife and walked towards him. He was screaming through the rag in his mouth, the muscles in his body trying to expand enough to burst the straps holding him down. Completely futile efforts, as Malcolm dug the blade into his throat, pulling back in a slow-motion instantly turning the muffled screams to gurgles. Blood soaking the rag from his mouth, and shooting into the air from the gaping wound in his neck. His body convulsed for about a minute, as the life sapped from him and his heart stopped. Martin, Michelle, and David were all crying on the gurneys behind him, there was no escape from this game for them.

Returning to the corner, Malcolm cleaned the knife with a rag and reached for his plastic sheeting. Laying this out on the floor, he began his ritual of removing the body from the gurney and wrapping it on the floor. Checking the spyhole, he opened the doors and carried the body to the Fiesta. The journey to dump the body took about twenty minutes this time, utilising as many back roads as he could and travelling about four miles in total. In a manner that he had become accustomed too, he dumped the body indiscriminately on a footpath on a quiet street and made the journey back to the container.

Parking the car and then closing the big steel door, he checked the restraints of his prisoners before laying the sleeping bag on the floor and settling in for the night. As he lay staring up at the makeshift ceiling, he thought about his sister, the journey where this all began. Her beautiful face floated in front of his eyes, still thirteen all these years on. How different their lives would have been if she hadn't been tormented, if she hadn't felt so bad that she had taken her own life from the top of a tower block. He hadn't been there for her in her darkest hour, but neither had anyone else. The systems designed to keep people safe were inadequate and broken. Bad people were allowed to get away with their bad actions. Sleep came quickly for him despite the cries from the gurneys.

1993

Jimboy and his mates were hanging about at the bottom of the tower block stairwell, one of them spraying a tag on the brick wall behind them, and the rest just generally mucking about, sharing a bottle of White Lightning between them.

"Hold up," Jimboy announced, "here comes that prick Malcolm." Across the courtyard, the skinny young lad had been heading to the stairwell looking for his sister. He had been home, seen his drunk mother, and realised Isabella had been there, collected the pound coin, and left. He figured she'd be at the top of the stairs. As he began to cross the courtyard he heard the call from Jimboy and looked up at the seven lads. He paused briefly, thinking about the right course of action. He really wanted to see if his sister was at the top of the tower, but he didn't want to have to go through them.

"I'm bored," said Jim to his friends, "wanna have some fun?" The guys he was with agreed, and as a group, they started moving towards Malcolm, who had stopped about twenty feet away. Malcolm wanted to be brave, but he was skinny and not very good with his fists. Although he was brave, he was no match for the seven lads walking towards him. He had to think quickly, he knew he was pretty fast, the logical option was to outrun them and then circle back to the tower when he had managed to lose them. His mind made up, he turned one hundred and eighty degrees and took off as fast as his feet would move. "It's on," shouted Jim, and he and his gang took off after the skinny lad.

Darting from street to street, Malcolm was not as fast as he thought, with the lads closing in on him as he began to tire. Soon they were inches behind him he realised he was in serious trouble, he was afraid, but he was also brave. He knew he would have to land a couple of punches, and maybe that would be enough to limit the beating. The eight boys circled him, Jimboy standing just a few feet in front of him. "What is it prick?" said Jimboy, catching his breath "think you can take all of us?" One of the lads behind Malcolm shoved him in the back, making him lunge forward towards Jimboy, with Jimboy stepping deftly to the side and landing a punch on the back of Malcolm's head. Instinctively stretching his hands out in front of him to break his fall, Malcolm managed to prevent his head from hitting the ground. He lifted himself off the ground and the group repositioned themselves to keep the boy in the middle of the circle. "Think you can take me?" taunted Jimboy, "come on, take your best shot."

Malcolm looked briefly around the group of boys, and then back at Jim. He knew he was going to be hurt but he was brave enough to defend himself. Standing a few feet from Jim, he clenched his fist and took a swing at his aggressor's face. It was easily deflected by the stronger Jimboy, who took his own swing, connecting cleanly with Malcolm's nose, causing a rapturous cheer from the gang. Malcolm hit the deck, followed swiftly by a boot from Jimboy in the gut before the other seven boys began to use their feet.

A few moments later, the street was illuminated by the blue flash of a police car's lights, and an ear-piercing screech of the siren. Two uniformed officers climbed out of their patrol car and began running over to the fight. Spotting them Jimboy shouted, "Pigs, clear out," and began running in the opposite direction, along with the boys, leaving Malcolm laying on the ground holding onto his stomach and curled up in a ball, spitting blood from his mouth. The officers gave chase and managed to tackle two of Jimboy's gang to the ground, restraining them in cuffs and arresting them.

While the officers waited for a police van to arrive to take the two attackers to the cells for questioning, they placed Malcolm in the back of the squad car, checking that his injuries were not too severe. He sat in the back seat, his nose throbbing, and his head pounding, and watched as the van arrived as two of his attackers were taken away. The officers climbed into the car and began driving back to their station. As they navigated the streets the car passed the courtyard to the tower block. They rounded the corner and Malcolm spotted his sister, Isabella, looking directly at him. He could see she had been crying and he pleaded with the officers to stop so he could see her, but they ignored his requests and continued on their journey.

Friday, April 14th, 7.30am

In the Ops room the following morning Jim and Brad were there early but were still beaten by half a dozen officers. The serious nature of the missing detective had sparked a fresh incentive to speed up the search for Malcolm. There was now no doubt that Malcolm was behind Ash's disappearance, but how they were not sure. The search area had been widened to pretty much all of South London, and they were literally banking all their efforts on the door to door searches.

Gregory's body had been found at about 4am by a taxi driver. It was already in the morgue, with the street being cordoned off from the media who had swooped on the area. Residents had been woken during the night by police constables looking for any clues possible, and CCTV in the area was being scanned for any sign of a possible vehicle.

Jim and Brad drank coffee, co-ordinating what they could from their desks. Brad had phoned Lisa on the way into work in the morning, her mother had answered, allowing Lisa to rest, advising him that a doctor was on the way to give her and the baby a check-up. Jim had already been on the phone to Alison giving her an update on the case and receiving feedback on the widespread riots.

They were waiting on the YouTube video being released, now expected to prep the public on the type of person who Martin Imbeault would be either condemning or protecting. Brad hung up the phone he had been conversing on. "Martin Imbeault is coming into the Yard boss," he said, looking at Jim, "he's being brought in by uniform and he's alone."

Jim leant back in his chair, "What do you think he'll do?"

Brad drew a breath, "Difficult one," he exhaled, "he's guilty as fuck and has gotten away with systematic abuse of minors for years. Donna, his wife has had his back all this time, either through blind loyalty or complete ignorance." He stood up to pour another coffee from the percolator. "However, by the time he sits in that chair Malcolm will no doubt have told the British public about his acts, which might tip him over the edge."

Scanning the room to ensure no one was within earshot, "I fucking hope his brains end up on the pavement," said Jim. He had reached a point in the week where his logic told him they were not catching Malcolm unless they got lucky. But part of him agreed with Malcolm, people had become far too immune to the horrors that were going on in the world, and the police were too ill-equipped to deal with it.

With that, a Junior Detective brought over an iPad, "He's posted," he stated and he placed the screen on the desk and pressed play.

"Good Morning Britain. The gorgeous Claire Papadoplous decided not to show up last night and so the police found her partner Gregory with his throat slit this morning. To be fair, she was not my most precious victim, but a nice little filler just to make the rest of her life a recurring trip to counselling.

"Now, we have a much more interesting story tonight. I have asked Martin Imbeault to sit in my chair tonight. Martin's wife, Donna, is with me here and I am not sure she is totally innocent either. You see, Malcolm is a prolific sex offender, abusing many boys over the years while he worked in a youth centre and coached a junior football team. The police were unable to make anything stick, and his wife certainly used to cover for him. And before the media run the story using the word "alleged" before paedophile, let's just ensure there is no doubt. This is not guesswork on my part, or me listening to rumours, Martin abused me for two years when I was just twelve years old and in a very lonely place in my life.

"Malcolm will sit in that chair, and he will decide whether to punish himself, or live a life looking over his shoulder."

With that, the video ended. "Shit," exclaimed Jim, "I know him!" He stood up quickly, looking at Brad with wide eyes. A memory had been dislodged when he heard Malcolm say that final phrase. "Living a life looking over his shoulder." A phrase he had heard some twenty-five years ago.

"You going to share?" Brad questioned.

"It can't be him," Jim sat back down, staring directly at Brad, "when I was young, about fifteen, I was not the character I am now, I was a little thug, and I ran with a group of kids that pretty much all ended up on the wrong side of the law. Fuck, no, I'm bullshitting myself." He took a deep breath, before confessing to himself and to Brad. "I was the ring leader, we were a bunch of fucking cretins, knocking around the Crossways Estate. Hooligans with no future, spray painting, petty vandalism, drinking …" he paused, shifting in his seat. The man, confident in his age and his profession, suddenly felt very, very guilty. Brad's kept his face straight, he'd never seen Jim like this. "Well there was this girl, about twelve, we got a kick out of tormenting her, and we got pretty bad with it. We used to corner her in the stairwell of one of the towers, used to rough her up, burn her hair, we had a run-in with her brother a couple of times."

"Malcolm?" Brad offered.

"Yeah, Malcolm. But it didn't end there…" his eyes widened even more, "Jesus Christ! That's where I knew Nicola from." The memories were forming now as he began to recall his story to Brad. "Isabella. That was her name, Nicola used to hang around with my gang occasionally. She was involved when we use to pick on Isabella. Fuck … his sister committed suicide."

"Fuck sake Jim," exclaimed Brad, "are you sure it's our Malcolm."

"Povey, that wasn't his surname, get checking but I think it was Steele back then. His sister, Izzy, she committed suicide on a night I had a fight with Malcolm. There was this guy who was questioned." Jim paused, sitting at his desk, he slowly turned his head to the board that Ash had built. Standing up from his seat he walked towards it. "No fucking way." He was looking at the picture of Darren Alderman, "it's him."

Brad had stood from his chair and walked over to stand beside Jim, "You're confusing me guv."

Jim didn't turn away from the board, "The girl Isabella, apparently, she was raped, and took a dive off the tower block. That guy Darren, I know him too, he was at my school, and everyone knew he had done it." Jim cleared his throat, "Darren raped Malcolm's sister, we beat her up, we beat him up, and she committed suicide. Afterward, that lad went mental, he tried to come after us all, starting fights, even tried to start one with me. Not long after that my parents moved and had me off to college." He turned to look at his colleague, "Brad, we killed that little girl, and her brother faced up to us all, the last thing I ever heard him say was 'You'll be looking over your shoulder for the rest of your life.' It's him, that lad is Malcolm."

Brad sat still for a moment, a million things he could be saying to Jim right now, a million things that would not help. He chose his words carefully, "How does that help us stop him, Jim?" Jim raised an eyebrow to Brad. "Seriously, shit happens which we'll deal with later, but right now I don't see how that changes the facts."

"Malcolm will know it's me heading the case, Christ he probably even banked on it, a serious case like this was bound to be handed to the senior DCI." Jim paused, wondering what to do next. Ash was missing, four nights had passed since Malcolm announced his game, a paedophile was about to take the stage tonight, riots all over Britain, and suddenly he felt like he was cast even further into the mess. "They are all linked, somehow. Get the team looking into the name 'Isabelle Grant', and start looking for further connections into that case."

"Boss," Brad leant a little closer, "What will they find about you?"

It was a good question, and Jim knew the answer. The investigation following the suicide turned up nothing. The police spoke to Jim's parents, his family came from a nicer neck of the woods, they didn't look too deep, and it wasn't long before Jim was finished college and completing the application to be a police officer. The saga was forgotten by Jim's family and buried in the deep recesses of his own memories. "Nothing," said Jim, "That's why Malcolm is involving the police, he wants to show our limitations."

1990

As the coach's whistle rang out across the gym hall the kids playing the match lined up to shake the hands of the opposing team. With the game over the players began to disappear with their parents, the chattering of goal scores filling the auditorium and Dad's high fiving their sons and daughters.

"It's late Malcolm," called out the coach to the boy stood with no parent, "give me a hand putting the balls away and I'll give you a lift."

The young lad looked up at the coach. "Its ok coach, you don't have to, I'll still put them away." He leaned down and scooped up two footballs, feeding them into the black netted bag with the others. The coach walked over, and started picking up the balls as well.

"Malcolm," the coach crouched down next to him, "come on, I'll give you a lift, it's cold out, and we could even get some chips on the way."

The boy paused. Chips would be nice he thought, all that was in the cupboards at home were tins of beans and super noodles. His Mum was a drunk, spent all of her social on vodka, with a sparse few quid for food. "Can I get some for my sister, coach?" He said as he placed the last ball in the bag.

"Sure, why not," the coach stood up, "and while the other kids aren't around you can call me Martin." Placing the last black bag in the kit cupboard and locking it, the two headed out of the hall and up the corridor, past reception and out into the cold November air.

Walking through the carpark Martin clicked his fob and the lights of a Porsche Boxter lit up, as did Malcolm's eyes.

"That's your car," Malcolm gawped, "you're shitting me!" Straight away Malcolm cupped his hand to his mouth, swearing in front of the coach was not allowed.

Martin looked at him and laughed, "Fuck yeah it's my car," he gestured to get in and gave the lad a wink. As Malcolm slammed the car door he eyes scanned the dash as his coach turned the key in the ignition. "Seatbelt, mate, come on I'll show you how fast it goes." Launching out of the carpark Martin spent the next half an hour speeding down dual carriageways, getting the tail out around roundabouts and listening to the laughter of the ten-year-old boy sitting in the passenger seat.

He pulled up outside a chip shop, pulling up the handbrake with a satisfying click. "Come on," he looked at Malcolm, "you pick whatever you want." With a smile on his face that was now starting to hurt, Malcolm climbed out of the car and walked into the chippy, staring up and the counter. His father was unknown and his mother was a drunk, standing in a chip shop with free choice was like Charlie Bucket finding the golden ticket to Wonka's factory.

"Savaloy and chips please, Coach," he looked up at him, "if that's ok?"

"Of course it is mate," the smile from his coach was comforting, "and what about for your sister?"

Malcolm looked back up at the board, "Erm …" he pondered, there was so much choice he couldn't think of anything. "Can she have the same?"

Martin smiled, looking towards the young girl taking the orders, "Three Savaloy and chips love, everything on them, and three tins of coke."

Back in the car, Martin drove away from the chip shop, "get stuck in, mate, I'll find somewhere to pull over and eat mine." Malcolm unfolded the paper and took the wooden fork between his thumb and forefinger, digging into the chips as Martin pulled into an empty carpark. Switching off the engine they were in almost darkness, except the glow of the blue lights on the dashboard. Martin grabbed his package of food from the back seat and tucked in. "So," he began with a mouthful of chips, "you're mum, she doesn't come to the games?"

Malcolm stopped chewing as he thought about what his mum was probably doing. Laying on the couch, a fag in one hand, wearing a dressing gown over tracksuit bottoms, drinking vodka and coke. She was a mess, even at ten years old he knew it, and he spent most of his time looking after Isabella, his little sister. It was him that made sure they got to school most days, it was him that fixed her sandwiches in the morning, even if it was just jam or peanut butter. His mum was a waste, drunk most of the time until she needed to go sign on the dole. He began to chew again and answered his coach, "meh, she doesn't like football."

"Well that's a shame mate, you're a fucking good little player." Martin picked up his Savaloy and took a big bite off the end, "you want some extra practice?"

Malcolm looked up at him, "what you mean coach?"

"Call me Martin," he looked down at you small boy, "well you're a good player, but with a bit more practice you could be really good." Malcolm smiled, he wanted to be like Gascoigne and play for England one day, at Wembley, lifting the World Cup.

"I don't know," he said, "My mum needs me at home quite a lot and I think the only reason she allows me to go is cos it's free at the youth club, she can't afford anymore."

"Don't be daft Malcolm," he put his hand on the boy's shoulder. "Listen I have scouts coming to the game next month, I could coach you for free, what you say?"

"You'd do that for me?" Malcolm wasn't used to having people be nice to him. He bit into his Savaloy, Martin's hand still resting on his shoulder.

"You're a special kid mate, I like you," squeezing his hand on his shoulder gently. "And if I can make you a better player, you can help me out a bit as a favour. What you say?"

Malcolm stopped chewing, feeling the hand on his shoulder start to rub up and down his arm. "I think I should go home."

"Oh sure," Martin removed his hand from the boy's shoulder. He folded his chip papers and put them on the back seat, "I can drop you back soon, but those scouts are only going to be interested in the most talented boys." He leaned over and placed his hand on Malcolm's thigh, his bare skin not covered by his shorts. He took Malcolm's small hand, the boy was trembling as he did, and he slowly slid it over the handbrake. As he did so, his other hand tugged at the waist of his own tracksuit bottoms, pulling his cock from his pants.

Friday, April 14th, 5pm

Harry strolled down the street. Although his father was dead, and his body had not been released from the morgue, he had been able to arrange the death certificate. He was heading to his solicitor's office to take care of the will, which would release his father's savings into his bank account. As his father was now dead the pension and benefits would stop, but his father's last will and testament left a sizable fortune to his son Harry, and he wanted to ensure he could cash out quickly. In the couple of days since his father was murdered, he received numerous threats on Facebook and Twitter, to the point where he had deleted his accounts. As brave and cocky as he was, the messages he was receiving were worrying. He knew he could handle himself if anyone did try to attack him, and he wasn't regretting his actions, but maybe with this cash from his inheritance he could move somewhere he was recognised a little less.

The police had decided not to hold him after his solicitor had made a good case for bail conditions. Harry had no criminal record, and as his father was alive he wasn't exactly cheating on his benefits. The charge had been left with false imprisonment, which the solicitor felt confident would be dropped eventually. After being offered some protection by a couple of uniforms, Harry had laughed, stating he didn't need babysitting. Returning home he had also started to strip the contents out of his father's bedroom and had spoken to an estate agent to book in a valuation. Sell up and move on was his only thought, just a matter of paperwork now.

He had left the city offices where he had registered the death of his father, the Registrar had not been courteous to him, recognising him from the news a few nights ago. He thanked her sarcastically and now walked with an A4 envelope in his hand to a pre-arranged appointment to have his fathers will read. Ahead of him, a man with a shaved head stood in the middle of the path staring directly at him, the lower part of his face covered with a bandana. Harry spotted him about twenty feet away and stopped walking. This guy was big, muscular, and he was there for a reason.

"Hey Harry," the man shouted, and suddenly Harry didn't feel as brave as he thought he would. He stepped back and had intended to turn, thinking he should cross the street, but as he stepped back he bumped into someone. Behind him was a man, again with a shaved head and a bandana, and again a sizable figure. Harry spun round to look at him and noticed about a dozen men crossing from the other side of the street. Most had shaved heads, faces covered, wearing denim jeans, t-shirts, tattoos and all looking like they wanted to kill him.

Harry was speechless as, in broad daylight, the man that had been stood behind Harry punched him hard in the face, breaking his nose instantly. The man that had initially blocked Harry's path approached at speed, using his steel toe cap boots and a running kick to connect with Harry's temple, cracking his eye socket and dislodging his eye. The two men dragged Harry by the shoulders into the middle of the street, passers-by stood watching, moving themselves back into shop doorways. In the middle of the street, they dropped Harry who was barely conscious, such was the force of the punch and the kick he had just received. Blood was pouring down from his nose over his mouth.

One by one the masked men attacked Harry as he lay whimpering. Some hit him with their fists, some with feet, and some with wooden bats or knuckle dusters. The attack was grim. Harry's face was a mess, dozens of cuts, dislocated jaw, his left eye hung down by his broken cheekbone. His arm had been snapped in two, with his forearm bent back on itself. The ordeal lasted for five minutes.

The two men that had first attacked Harry retreated to a black van parked at the side of the road. The rest of the men began to disappear, into alleyways or side streets. As the engine of the van came to life, a woman began to approach the man that was laying in his own blood. The horn of the van was blasted, and the woman stepped back towards the curb, as the accelerator was floored, and the van roared down the street towards Harry. As the woman screamed, Harry managed to open his eye as the front of the van connected with his face, the wheels ripping over his body, and continuing on its journey before disappearing around a bend.

Friday, April 14th, 6pm

Jim entered the room where Martin Imbeault was sitting, closely followed by Brad. They hadn't offered him the relative comfort of the family room, instead, treating him to the sterile interview room. A duty officer stood in the corner of the room. As Jim entered Martin began to protest, "Detective this is insane, people are dying…"

"Enough Mr. Imbeault," Jim said sternly, "It's 6pm, and we have been unable to locate your wife, the other two hostages, or our missing Detective." Jim paused a moment, allowing Martin to spout.

"This is a fucking joke," as he spoke, he was clearly shaking, "You are really telling me that I pay my taxes to sit…"

"ENOUGH!" Brad bellowed from the pit of his stomach, he hated this man, this vile human being that was sat before him. Jim nodded to the Duty Sergeant who left the room. "What the fuck do you think is going on here you little prick." Martin, stumped, tried to offer a mutter of objection, but a sudden glare from Jim told him to shut his mouth. "There is a fucking psycho out there that some years ago you had a part in creating. A fucking psycho that is holding your wife hostage and has proven he will kill her if you are still breathing air at 9pm." Brad had allowed his voice to get very loud.

Jim had sat quiet, almost flinching when Brad told Martin that he had helped create a psycho, he could now include himself in that statement. "Mr. Imbeault," Jim was calm, classic good cop, bad cop, "I can't tell you what to do, but consider this, all three of us here know you are a kiddie fiddler, and if you are alive at 9pm you'll be arrested, prosecuted and left to fend for yourself. So it's up to you." He stood up, shrugging his shoulders. "Your wife, not sure if you love her, but her life is in your hands, and your future is in ours." With that, the two men walked out of the room. "Keep an eye on him," Jim said to the Duty Sergeant who had waited in the corridor, "You have my permission to keep him here at all costs." The Duty Sergeant smirked and the two detectives walked away.

They were approaching the Ops Room as a female officer opened the door "Guv, there's been a development." As the two men entered the room, there was a definite commotion, they flicked their eyes to the TV screen. The headline displayed in red:

BREAKING NEWS: Body found suspected to be that of Harry Singh

"What the fuck," Jim declared out loud, "how am I just hearing about this?" he demanded.

The female officer offered "We think he was attacked by a vigilante group, and the media were there before we were." Jim looked at the screen, police were arriving and beginning to cordon off the area, but the graphic scene of a body lying in the middle of the road was visible and he could hear the anchor advising viewers that the scenes may be distressing.

"Jesus fucking Christ," Jim turned to Brad, "what the fuck is happening?" Before Brad could answer Jim felt his phone vibrating, instantly knowing it would be Alison.

"My office, now!" The call ended abruptly.

"Brad, sort this shit out," and with that Jim left the room. It was a five-minute walk along corridors and lifts to get to Alison's office. It felt like an hour, he was failing to make any headway into the case, and now more people were dying. His mind had been wrestling with Malcolm's ethics all week, but today he was feeling guilty. The man had planned such a terrible event to avenge the people who did him wrong, to punish them by either ending their lives or taking their loved ones and publicly shaming them so their lives would not be the same again. These random strangers were linked by the six degrees of separation to this man who had been beaten by life so hard he had broken. And he was linked as well. He had been such a monster to that young girl, and the fact that she had taken her own life had devastated Malcolm, while he continued on with his own, eventually becoming a detective at the top of his game. And now he was tasked with finding the man tearing the moral fibre of the country apart, exposing the weaknesses in the system that allows so many morally corrupt people to survive and thrive. Maybe this was his punishment, he thought, Malcolm had been left without a sister and the boy had no one listening to him, and here he was, a detective with the eyes of the world on him and not one single answer of how to save anyone. Touché he thought. He had reached Alison's door, taking a deep breath and preparing himself for a roasting, he entered.

Friday, April 14th, 8.45pm

Martin sat in the rear passenger seat behind the driver, his face was white, and he was quiet. He had been allowed to watch the news reports of the guy Harry being killed in broad daylight by a gang of thugs. His mind was a swirl, a hurricane blew around his thoughts, and nothing cohesive was allowed to form. He was losing his mind, thinking about the children he abused, thinking about Malcolm. Before this week these memories were precious to him, they would form in his mind when he lay with his wife, Donna, he would use those memories for his pleasure, but now they were causing him pain. He didn't spend much time thinking about Donna, as his mind kept flashing to the image of the dead man, Harry, in the street. Imagining himself being chased and caught was terrifying. Self-preservation was clashing in his mind and he was panicking, sweating and breathing deeply. He glanced over briefly at DCI Ford who sat next to him, and his colleague Burnham in the front, those two men wanted him dead, they wanted to save the innocent people, and he was certainly not one of them.

He looked again at Jim. "I did it," he uttered quietly, catching Jim's attention. Brad looked at him through the reflection of the mirror in the passenger visor. Martin didn't wait for a response, this burden on his chest was weighing him down like never before. He had been attacked before, it was terrifying, but he had always known it would just be a few bruises and that they would heal. This was different, there were people out there who would do more than just punch him. "Over the years there were more than a dozen," he began to weep, "I don't know why it started, but I couldn't stop. They were all so young." He hung his head low, he wasn't making much noise.

Jim glanced at Brad, neither of them needed to say anything. They just hoped that Malcolm would be dropping off his wife, breathing and well in a couple of hours. For the next five minutes, Martin said nothing and moved less. They arrived at the familiar scene of Trafalgar Square, the noise again deafening but it felt louder than ever. As the two detectives exited the car they caught the chill of the April evening. There was a slight breeze, the rain was beginning to fall and the grey pavement slabs were already wet from recent showers. Glancing at his watch Jim advised Brad they had five minutes. Brad went around to the passenger side door, opened it and leant in. Martin briefly looked up, "You ready?" Brad asked. Despite his contempt for this man in the back seat of the BMW, he understood the gravity of the situation and was not going to return to the anger he displayed earlier this evening. Placing his hand on Martin's elbow, he helped him out of the car. The now-familiar roar from the crowd filled the air and did not subside. It was like a Roman crowd cheering as their favourite gladiator wounded his victim, perhaps severing a limb. It would not be long before the fight would be over, but Brad could still not predict the outcome.

Martin stood, the shake in his legs nearly toppled him and Brad held him firmly. "Can you walk?" Brad asked.

Martin took a moment, "I'm ok." He gathered his strength, trying to control the adrenaline in his body. Hearing the taunts from the crowd, he began to understand just how much he was hated. As he walked to the chair, he thought again about the dead man, Harry. Then something spurred in his memory which made him stop about ten feet from the chair. He worried for his wife, the thugs that would surely kill him, that killed Harry, what they would think of her? A victim or an accomplice? He turned quickly and faced the two detectives who about twenty feet away, "How long have I got?" he shouted.

Jim looked at his watch, "Two minutes." he shouted back, and then glanced curiously at Brad. The game was out of their hands now, but he had no clue what he was doing. Martin turned to the cameras, they had been moved much farther away than when Nicola Johnston had addressed them before saving her son's life.

"I'M GUILTY," he shouted loudly. With almost instantaneous impact, the crowd became very quiet. Martin paused briefly as he looked around, "I'M GUILTY. I PREYED ON THOSE INNOCENT BOYS, I DID IT. BUT MY WIFE, SHE KNEW NOTHING, I HID IT … SHE IS A GOOD WOMAN. PLEASE, PLEASE LEAVE HER ALONE." There was a moment of humanity being offered from a man who had lived a life of total sin. An evil, predatory man, who, finally tried to do something decent with his actions.

He turned from the cameras and started walking slowly to the chair. Seeing the gun within inches he reached for it. The rain pooled on the seat, as he lifted the gun and sat down. His head hung low, the crowd had remained quiet. The bell struck and Martin froze. He did not move. It rang out for a second time, and still, he froze. He pictured Malcolm as a boy, he saw the fear in the boy's eyes, sat across from him in the passenger seat of his car. His final memory as he lifted the gun, placing the ice-cold barrel in his mouth and pulled back on the trigger.

Friday, April 14th 9.10pm

Malcolm sat looking at the BBC news channel on the iPad. The light from it once again cast flickering shadows over the three gurneys in the room. He could hear Donna crying from beneath her gag, and looked at the bottle of chloroform sat on the shelf. His predator was dead, taken his own life in what appeared to be the only act of selflessness he had ever displayed. He had saved his wife, and with his performance before pulling the trigger, had quite possibly saved her a lifetime of torment.

As the news cameras continued to show the scene, paramedics checking on the corpse, a private ambulance reversing up to the scene, and a trained officer making the gun temporarily safe, he sat and watched DCI Ford getting into his car, leaving the scene. He had intended something different for Jimboy, but in his own mind, a new plan began to form, one that he liked very much. He stretched out for his facemask, placed it over his nose and mouth and picked up the bottle of chloroform and a rag. Unscrewing the top he doused the rag and walked the few feet to Donna. The smell inside the container was almost unbearable now, Malcolm had been using a bucket in the corner to limit the chances of being spotted, and the victims had not had the dignity of a bathroom break since Sunday night, so they lay in their own embarrassments. "Widow Donna," he said coldly through his mask, "hopefully you now see who your husband truly was." He placed the rag over her mouth.

About an hour later, Malcolm was driving the Fiesta through the back streets of London. His game was changing, something he had not planned for but he felt this was an improvement. Parking the car after about twenty minutes he climbed out of the driver's seat after checking the street was truly quiet. He walked to the back of the car and lifted the boot lid as quietly as he could. He had decided to use the car which meant that squeezing the bodies into it was more difficult, but he figured much less chance of being spotted. After lifting the two, breathing, bodies out of the car, he dragged them both onto the footpath, before returning to the rear of the car and closing the boot lid quietly. Looking back at the two bodies, wrapped in plastic, with the rain bouncing off of them, he grinned, checked the street to make sure he hadn't been spotted, and returned to the yard.

Saturday, April 15th, 7.30am

"Boss!" Brad nudged Jim's arm. His eyes opened, heavy from only a couple of hour's sleep. The family sofa was not comfortable, but it had been enough. Brad offered a coffee in one hand as Jim swung his legs around and sat up. At thirty-eight, he was not equipped to multiple late nights, no matter how young he told himself he was. He took the cup from Brad, looking at his other hand and noticing the iPad.

"Ok, play it." He breathed in deep and exhaled, sipping the hot coffee. Malcolm's voice played as expected.

"The number of times a parent was told by the police that they had no evidence and they could not follow up on enquiries is a testament to the way the police force is run and the laws that they enforce." For the first time, Malcolm's voice was delivered with a softer tone, no sarcasm or entitlement came through on this video. "I have planned this week for years, and the sense of justification from tonight's suicide is surging through me. Years of not being believed, and finally he has confessed, and in the process saved his wife. I urge the public to support Donna Imbeault and not to condemn her. She was innocent, a pawn in her husband's sick life, she was innocent like we were innocent. When I designed this game, I thought I should have a control group and so I had taken Michelle, knowing her and her father are good people. I expected that no one would have made the ultimate sacrifice, and I would need to prove what good people will do. But I have proved that, beyond a shadow of a doubt, some bad people can have moments of good in them. So now I have learned that, Donna and Michelle have been released." With that Jim snapped his head to look at Brad, he was nodding with a forced smile on his face. The video continued, "Michael and David. Now, these two are an interesting couple, model citizens, charity workers, loved by the public, adored by the rich and famous, hell, they even ran with an Olympic torch. But they are crooked, you see, they set up the Samuel Higgins Trust for a little boy who died of cancer. They put some of the money towards charity, but line their pockets heavily with fat salaries. Total scum. And I have a big issue with that," the blurry screen cut to a newspaper article, zooming slowly in on the picture. It showed the boy Samuel Higgins, in a hospital bed, with the two men Michael and David stood next to him. "You see, here they are, smiling for the press," the picture continued to zoom in, scanning to the right of the two men, tracing up the head of the bed. Stood right next to the sick boy was another young boy, a boy who was not smiling in the picture, "and that little boy is me. Samuel Higgins was my best friend. And they use his name to drive around in Maserati's and live in Westend apartments. Michael, the game is yours, see you at 9."

The video stopped.

"Fuck," Jim breathed out, "we seriously have Michelle and Donna?"

"Alive and well boss," said Brad, "The girl's father Roy is heading to the hospital as we speak, and Donna has had her brother arrive."

"Ash?" Jim inflected his voice quietly.

Brad gently shook his head, "still nothing." Jim stood up, stretching his back and gulping his coffee.

"Our week has been shortened by a day," Jim clocked the time at 7.30am, "David Sutherland?"

"Uniforms are bringing him from their home now. We'll sit on him as best as we can but he's lawyered up." Brad opened the door for Jim as they both moved into the hallway, "You need a shower boss. You smell like you've slept on a couch."

"Thanks for the confidence boost," Jim gave Brad a once up and down, "You're hardly model material mate. I want to speak to Donna."

On the drive to the hospital, Jim thought about the previous five nights. George, the cowardly abuser, who probably didn't realise how real Malcolm was and how real his threat, who chose his life over his victim. Nicola, who pulled the trigger to save the son that everyone had forgotten and given up on. Harry, the most dismissive of all, not caring for his father and not ashamed of showing it, joining his father in death at the hands of the public he taunted. Claire, the serial user of men, not the worst of sins but she played with the wrong guy, and ran away when her time was called. And Martin, the child abuser, finally pushed into the corner of confession, saving his wife by sacrificing his own life.

Donna and Michelle were alive, most likely traumatised, but breathing. Jim thought about Malcolm's decision to release Michelle. Jim had truly expected this to go to the end, and he had even prepared his final chat with Roy Ritchie, and the fact he no longer had to deliver it was a relief. He instantly liked that man and knew early on that he would swallow a bullet. Michael was next, the big question, who would be in a body bag tonight?

As they walked along the corridor they saw two uniforms stood at the entrance to a private ward. Jim had decided to speak to

Michelle, he assumed that Donna would be too distraught, and hoped Michelle would be a little more lucid with the information. As they entered Roy greeted him.

"Detectives," Roy said, gripping Jim's hand firmly first, then Brad's, "Not much I can say, we got lucky, but thank you. Have you found your colleague?"

"Not yet," replied Jim, "Can we speak with your daughter, sir?"

"Of course, she's just had a shower, that bastard ..." Roy tensed up, "Please." Roy ushered his hand toward the curtain surrounding the bed.

As Jim pulled the curtain back slightly, he and Brad stepped inside. "Nice to meet you, Michelle," he offered.

She looked pale and had been crying recently. "Detectives, please come in," Michelle spoke well considering her ordeal. Jim could sense her father's strength in her. She had been tied down to a gurney for five days, fed little and forced to soil herself, and yet her voice was calm and collected, "My Dad mentioned you, thank you for looking for me."

"Michelle, it's good to see you well, and I know you have been through such a terrible ordeal," said Jim.

"Please Detective, I'm ok, ask your questions, there is still a man out there," Michelle's strength shone through. "I'm sure I'll freak out later, but I hope I can help."

Jim smiled, "What can you tell us?"

"He moved us, on the second night after he released Chris. We were in a basement before then, and he put us to sleep after he let him live. I woke up in a container, I think maybe we were at the docks. I think he had boarded up the inside of it, but I could hear the creaks of the doors as he came and went." She took a sip of water before continuing, wiping her hand across her mouth which was still red from the gag she had been forced to wear all week. "He had everything he needed in there, a sleeping bag, iPads, food, and he didn't leave the container much. Sat on his stool watching the news most of the time, he left to …" she paused as she recalled him slitting the throat of Mr. Kalarahi and Gregory, "he left to move the bodies, and I presume in the morning he left to post the videos. He showed us everything he made and seemed to take great pleasure from it."

"Can you tell us any more about the container?" Brad asked. "Any detail could be important."

She paused, "There isn't much to say. It looked like it was plaster boarded, I couldn't hear a thing from outside. I'm sorry."

"Michelle, we found the basement that he kept you for the first two nights, and now we know we are looking for a container," Jim stood up, "thank you so much, I will come back and see you. If you need anything the officers here will get it for you, and if there is anything else that comes to mind please call me directly." Jim offered over his card. He turned to Roy, "Sir, thank you," he shook his hand and the two detectives left

As they walked down the corridor Jim took his phone from his pocket to call the Operations Room, "You think he's still at the docks?" Jim asked before he dialled.

"Jim he never was," Brad replied. Jim raised an eyebrow. "She mentioned an iPad that was playing a lot, he had power, and you don't get those kinds of containers at the docks."

"Shit," Jim rolled his eyes and pressed dial. "Start searching any storage yards which use metal shipping containers," he ordered as the phone rang, "start in the target area and work out quickly. There can't be that many."

Saturday, April 15th 12 noon

In the Ops Room, Brad slammed down the phone, "Get your jacket," he bellowed at Jim, realising he was talking with Alison who had come down from her office for a motivational chat. Jim spun round to see him sliding his arm into his own blazer, "Container yard, ten miles away, SWAT are on route, uniform at the scene."

"Tell them to keep their distance," Jim shouted, turning back to Alison, "cross your fingers." She nodded to him as he turned and followed Brad out of the office at pace.

With the blue lights on the BMW, Brad careened in between the traffic that had pulled to the side of the road. Coming up at various junctions he was muttering obscenities beneath his breath, whilst Jim was making various calls to sergeants who were also on route. The last call was from the SWAT commander, they were on-site and breaching. Jim hung up, "How long?"

"Five minutes boss if these cunts get out of the way," Brad was focussed, he wanted to find Ash for Lisa more than anything, and he was now allowing himself some hope.

As they pulled into the street there was already a half dozen cars and a van outside the entrance to the yard. Brad pulled on the handbrake and both men bolted from the car, running to the gates. As they approached armed officers were walking back out of the yard. They looked sombre, guns lowered to the ground. Jim and Brad both slowed to a trot as they cleared the gates and began to move down the gravel incline that formed the drive.

"JIM!" exclaimed Brad as he lay his eyes on Ash's car, "fuck, no."

Jim looked down toward four officers who were stood at the open doors of a container, full tactical gear on. He noticed the van behind, with an officer walking toward him. "Sorry, Jim, Brad," the officer said as they walked passed him. They reached the container, glancing in they saw abandoned gurneys, an officer inside inspecting the contents on a makeshift desk. Brad looked at Jim with real fear in his eyes. They walked passed the open metal doors towards two more officers who were looking at the two detectives. As they rounded the metal door the rear of the van came into view. The roller door was pushed up, and Ash's face looked at them, his body wrapped in polythene.

Brad dropped to his knees letting out a loud cry of anger, rage had been filling him and he let it out in an explosion. Jim's shoulders sunk, his breaths drew deep. He had failed. He looked down to his colleague, and placed a hand on his shoulder briefly, and then proceeded to take his jacket off. He stepped closer to the back of the van, looking at the open eyes of Ash's corpse, and laid the jacket over his face. Choking back his tears, he was determined he would not break with all of these officers watching. He turned and walked back to Brad, looking down he quietly ushered, "Up you get Brad."

The older man got to his feet slowly, taking a deep breath as he did. Using the sleeve of his blue jacket he dabbed his eyes and looked at Jim, "We've got to be the first to tell Lisa, Jim, I'm going there now, I need to do it face to face."

Jim nodded, "We'll go together."

"No Jim, you get to work," Brad shook his head, "I'll be fine and I won't be long." Brad looked around, "Plenty of men here to take you back to the yard. I'll see you there in a couple of hours." As he began to walk away he turned briefly, "I'll be alright boss, you?" Jim nodded and Brad left the yard.

Dialling Alison's number on his phone, he listened to the dial tone as he scanned the inside of the container. "Jim, talk to me."

"We found Ash," Jim had to take another deep breath after he said that, "it's not good ma'am."

"Fuck," Jim could almost hear Alison sit down as she said that, "that poor girl." She gave it a moment considering whether to dwell on that or get to talking business, "Where is he, Jim?"

"Bolted, must have been in his plan," Jim began walking up the drive, "He must have known releasing two prisoners would give us some more clues as to where he was. But now he only has one left, so it'll be easy for him to lay low until tonight." He signalled for one of the uniformed officers to drive him back and got a nod of agreement in return. Climbing into the passenger seat he continued, "Ma'am, we aren't going to find him."

"Jim, the fallout from this is going to be catastrophic, we might not get him before tonight but we need to be able to prove we have done everything we can," she paused, contemplating her next words carefully. "We need to do this for Ash and his baby, so if we don't get him tonight, this will be a case that will never go cold."

"Ma'am, I'll get him." Jim hung up.

Saturday, April 15th 12.30pm

Wearing his wig and hoody, Malcolm sat in his fiesta. As the BMW drove passed him, with DCI Ford and Burnham heading to the container yard, he tilted his wing mirror and rearview so he could see the car. This was the riskiest move he had made all week and had not been part of his original plan. He had moved David Sutherland to a small outhouse at the Sireon yard where he used to work. It was a Friday night when he moved him, and he knew no one would be back there until Monday morning. Although not soundproofed like the cellar or the container, it wasn't within earshot of any worries and had a solid steel pipe that ran in and out of the ground, part of an old heating system. Having ditched the gurney, David was now handcuffed hand and foot around the pipe, and the gag had been replaced with some very tough silver gaffer tape, wrapped several times around his head, covering his mouth sufficiently. He had stayed long enough for David to come round from the chloroform and then drove back to the container yard, being sure to park just out of sight.

He had calculated that the focus would all be on the yard for a bit and that the uniforms would not go door to door for a while. Sitting with his phone ready to be placed to his ear as a kind of disguise, he figured he would go unnoticed. Watching the armed officers descend on the scene had almost made him turn the keys in the ignition and drive off, but as he sat there in plain sight and they drove passed he realised he was invisible. He had seen the two detectives arrive and after about fifteen minutes he saw the BMW drive in the opposite direction, slowing pulling out of his parking space he followed the car, remaining about twenty to thirty yards behind. As he approached several sets of lights his brain was working overdrive. What did he do if the car went through on green but he got stopped on red? What if the BMW got stopped on red and he had to pull up behind him?

He followed the car regardless of his paranoia, stopping at several lights, most of the time with a couple of cars between him and the detective. There was one set where he was directly behind, and his heart was racing. He half expected the driver door to be flung open at any moment and the big brutish detective to run up and pull him from the car. His hand hovered over the gear stick ready to shove it into reverse, but it was not needed. The light turned to amber, then green, and they were underway again. Keeping his distance he was courteous to a couple of cars pulling out of side streets, allowing them to drive in front of him but always keeping an eye on the detective.

Following through London he found himself heading to the suburbs and watched the BMW pull into a small communal parking area at a block of flats. He continued driving and pulled into the next side street, completing a U-turn after a dozen or so yards. As he drove back down to the junction he could see the detective entering through the main door, he drove slowly back onto the main road and pulled up a couple of hundred yards away, positioning his car so he could still see the front of the building. Retrieving his phone from the glove box, he entered the passcode and touched the photo folder. The first photo was a screenshot from Lisa Chilton's Facebook page, a lovely picture of the detective he had murdered and his fiancé celebrating them getting the keys to their first home. Dozens of likes and comments, but Malcolm wasn't interested in those. He placed two fingers on the screen and zoomed in. The picture was taken in front of the new door, Ash was holding Lisa in his arms like a newlywed bride, and over their shoulder was the number eight.

He sat for an hour, watching the door of the flats. Eventually, the detective left and headed to his car, making a call on his mobile as he did. Malcolm sat for another few minutes, and then pulled his car into the car park after watching the detective leave. Glancing around he got out of the car, lifting his rucksack, and walked the few paces to the front door. He pressed the buzzer for number three and hit call. After a few minutes, a voice answered, "Hello?"

"I have a package for number four," he called.

"Sure, there's a dropbox just inside," the voice replied followed by the click of the door indicating the magnetic lock was released. Malcolm opened the door and stepped inside. Malcolm looked at the entrance hallway, two apartments opposite each other, looking up the stairwell he figured she must be on the fourth floor. He climbed the stairs keeping as quiet as he could, passing a bicycle on the first landing and a pram on the second. As he reached the door with the number eight, he slid his hand into the pocket of his hoody and removed the tazer. He knocked on the door and waited.

After a few moments he heard the chain being released, his heart pumped fast again, as the door opened an older woman stood before him, he raised his arm quickly before she could react and tazered her in the shoulder. She let out a yelp, and fell to the floor, banging into the wall as she did. Malcolm stepped inside, it wasn't the person he was after. He cursed himself briefly, before hearing "Mum" coming from the living room. He panicked and stepped back out into the hallway, hiding just behind the wall.

"Mum!!" Lisa screamed, she had left the living room and entered the hallway. She crouched down quickly to check her mum slumped in the corner, as Malcolm appeared from his hiding place in the hallway and grabbed her tightly from behind, with his hand firmly over her mouth.

"Fight me and I'll kill your baby," he growled in her ear. She froze. "We're going to get up together, understand?" Lisa nodded her head briefly, Malcolm rose to his feet, lifting Lisa as he did. "Close the door." She had one arm free and pulled it over until it closed. Malcolm walked her into the living room, "Is anyone else here?" She shook her head. "Scream and I'll hurt you, I'm going to release my hand," she nodded again. She stood absolutely frozen, as he released his arms she cradled her baby instantly. He removed his rucksack from his back and withdrew a pair of handcuffs and a roll of gaffer tape. He stepped towards her and she flinched, sobbing loudly, but he grabbed her wrists and applied the cuffs.

He reached for the gaffer tape and she shouted "No," but he glared at her, going back to his rucksack and removing his knife. He looked at her again, petrified but she said nothing. Lifting the folded edge of the tape he wrapped it around her mouth four times. "Sit," he commanded, pointing at the couch. Her legs weak with the traumatic events of the last few minutes she stumbled, and collapsed to her knees, almost crawling the last couple of feet. Malcolm returned to the hallway, pressing the chib on the Yale lock and putting the chain back in place. He dragged the older woman by the ankle into the living room, retrieving another set of cuffs from the bag. Flipping the woman onto her front, he pulled her hands behind her back and cuffed them in place. With the tape, he gagged her and wrapped some around her ankles.

He stood up and looked at Lisa, "We're going for a little ride."

Saturday, April 15th, 8.50pm

"You're the only one left," Jim sat in the back of the car with Michael. The well-dressed man had become unshaven, wearing a shirt that was at least a day old, and had clearly been lacking sleep. The crowds at Trafalgar Square were enormous, tens of thousands lined the streets. The police needed to cordon off streets to allow access by car to the square. Throughout the day the headlines on the news had focussed only on this story. The death of Martin, the release of Donna and Michelle, and now the discovery of Ash's body. Riots had erupted during the day, keeping forces across the country busy, and the sense of frustration and anger was hanging in the air around Malcolm's chair.

Michael had hardly spoken all day when Jim went to speak to him this afternoon, he had no intention of trying to talk him round. He had given up caring whether the man sitting next to him fired his brains over the slabs, or if he bottled it and they cleaned up a pavement somewhere in London in the middle of the night. Jim had given up completely, they had searched for Malcolm all week and when they got close, Ash had lost his life. He just wanted to get through the night, and not have to sit at the square a single second longer than needed. "What time is it?" Michael asked quietly.

Jim looked at his watch, "Ten minutes," he replied. There was no soul in his voice as he spoke, no empathy which he had shown with Martin and Nicola. The guy he looked at was scum, he might not have abused anyone, or hit anyone, but he exploited the death of a young boy and enriched his own life, Jim did not care either way. He leaned back in the rear seat of the car, leaning his head up and sighed.

Michael looked over at him. "We all have sins Detective," he offered, there was a quiver in his voice "what's yours?"

Jim was looking at the roof lining of the car. He thought about the question but did not move his head, he knew what he had done, and he felt guilty that he had completely forgotten about it as he had gotten older. It was his burden and Malcolm's acts this week had stirred the memory, causing Jim to lose focus on his job. "Ignorance." He responded. It was the only word he could think of and he did not feel like embracing any conversation with Michael. Instead, he looked at his watch and turned his head to look at him, "Five minutes, time to get out." Michael retorted, a tear was welling in the corner of his left eye.

The driver in the front of the car got out and opened the rear door. Michael sat there for a few seconds, before moving his heavy legs from the car and standing up. He took a deep breath as the noise reached his ears, casting his eyes around the square over the thousands of people who were here to witness his actions. As he scanned the scene his eyes saw the chair for the first time, he placed his hand on the roof of the car to steady himself.

Rounding the car, he tried his best to walk tall. Having seen the footage from the previous nights he walked a few paces towards the chair and then stopped, turning to look back at the car. Jim was sitting in the back seat, Michael could just see him through the tinted glass. The detective was looking straight forward and made no signs that he was going to get out of the car. He turned and continued to the chair, unable to stop the tears from flowing down his cheeks. He loved his husband, and he loved their lives together. It had never been intentional to skim so much money from the charity but the lifestyle was addictive. It had gotten to a point that they didn't even know how much they were pocketing and how much went towards helping anyone, and until this week, if he was honest, neither of them really cared. It was a front, a way of doing very little and earning millions. At times the two of them had even joked about it between them as they enjoyed a drive in the Maserati or swam in a pool at the villa on the Riviera. Earlier in the week, he had seen the murder of the Indian man, Harry. The British public was vicious, and he knew that life would be difficult for him, even impossible. Then there would be the inevitable investigation, possibly arrest, jail, his reputation was already in pieces. He had looked for support from his friends during the week and had found little in the way of comfort. The realisation that money bought acquaintances not friends was never more obvious than the way he had been shunned since Malcolm released that video about them. It didn't matter that there were no facts, no smoke without fire he had thought. He imagined life after tonight, without the one person he truly loved, the one person who couldn't judge him. It looked like a lonely future.

He looked down at the chair. The gun was sitting on it, he had never held a firearm. Leaning down he picked it up, the sense of tunnel vision silenced the whole of the square. He was in a trance as he sat down. The gun was weightless in his hand. The crowd could not hear him say "I'm sorry," as he lifted the gun into his mouth. The flash of the barrel made his cheeks look like a flare going off, the back of his skull opened, and his neck cracked back, and immediately forward, folding at the waist, his body slumped forward, the gun hitting the ground as it remained with his hand clenched around the grip. As his broken skull hit the grey paving slabs, the chime of Big Ben rang out over London.

Jim sat back in the seat, not looking at the chair. He didn't care.

Sunday, April 17th, 8am

Jim woke in his armchair with the noise of his phone vibrating on the glass coffee table. The armchair was in its fully reclined position, Jim laying on his back, slowly opening his eyes, looking at the ceiling above him. The phone continued to vibrate and then stopped. A long groan escaped from Jim's mouth as his hand swung to the side of the chair and he pulled the leaver slowly to push him to an upright position. He leaned forward and looked down at the carpet, his elbows on his knees, rubbing his face with the palms of his hands. He glanced at the empty bottle of Grouse on the table next to the phone, and the empty glass next to it. The phone began to vibrate again.

"Shit," he uttered as he leaned forward sliding the phone with his fingertips into his palm, flipping it over and seeing Brad's name. He swiped his thumb, "Yup."

"Get up, and get in!" Brad sounded desperate.

"Did we get him?" Jim asked, but he knew it was the wrong question by the tone of Brad's voice and the words he had used.

"No, the cunts posted again …" Brad paused, the line was quiet as he struggled to form the sentence.

"Brad?" Jim's intuition knew this wasn't good.

"He's got Lisa, Jim, the cunts got Lisa!"

"Fuck!" Jim practically shouted but got cut off by Brad.

"Jim, he wants you," Brad sensed a silence would follow. "Jim, he posted another video. Lisa is in it, with her mouth gagged, and he has exposed you."

"What?"

"You and his sister, everyone knows, and now he wants you to make a choice," despair filled Brad's voice. Even with all his years of experience, the torment of this week had grown beyond belief, and even he found himself wondering what the fuck was going on. "It's not over, Jim."

Jim sat in silence for a second, the cloud of a hangover solid in his mind, it was too easy for this to be a dream that he was still in. "I'll head in now." As he said that there was a loud knock at the door, Jim's head popped up. "I'll be there in half an hour, Brad." He hung up and got to his feet. The curtains in his living room were not doing a good job of cutting out the light with a couple of shards of morning sun slicing the room in half, illuminating the dust in the air. Bang Bang.

"Fuck," he uttered as he stood there. What the fuck did Malcolm want? He knew the answer, a million scenarios filled his brain already, and most of them concluded with his brain on the cobbles. That poor girl though, she's pregnant, eight fucking months. And Ash is dead. And the public, they killed Harry, Michael was shunned by his friends and family. Would that happen to him for a mistake he made as an asshole teenager? The scenarios whizzed fast in his conscious thoughts, they'll get him today, a lucky break, but they hadn't been lucky all week, Malcolm was good, and he was patient, and he hadn't made a mistake all week.

BANG BANG.

"All fucking right," he bellowed towards the hallway, glancing in the mirror above the mantel, even in the gloomy light he could tell he looked like shit. He turned and headed to the door, tucking in what he could of his shirt as he did. Lifting the chain and the latch he opened the door, squinting his eyes as the April sun pierced his pupils.

"DCI Ford? What are you going to do tonight?" In front of Jim was a reporter with a camera recording right over his shoulder. The reporter, a young guy with a professional haircut and smart suit thrust a microphone with BBC on the sleeve towards Jim.

"Fuck, you moved quickly," replied Jim. He hesitated and glanced up the street spotting another camera being unloaded from a Sky News van. If he remained in the house the street would be filled with the media in minutes and he would be swarmed. A few seconds went by without Jim saying anything.

"Is it true, DCI Ford, that you drove Malcolm's sister to suicide?" The reporter was not going anywhere. Looking back into the hallway Jim saw his car keys in the bowl on the sideboard and his suit jacket hanging on the peg. He grabbed both before stepping out of the front door, swinging it closed behind him.

"No comment," he said clearly to the reporter as he descended the four concrete stairs at to the pavement and clicked the fob. The lights of his car flashed and he opened the driver door, throwing the jacket on the passenger seat and climbing in.

The eager reporter threw one more question at him. "Are you going to save that woman." That made Jim pause briefly and look at the young man for a second. It was a question he didn't have an answer to, but one that sent a chill down his spine, as he knew, unless they got lucky, there was only one way to save her and the baby. He slammed the door shut, started the engine, and headed out of the street.

On his way through London, his phone rang again. He saw Alison's name on the dashboard and hit the green phone button. "Alison."

"Jim, where are you?"

"On my way in, about twenty minutes," Jim turned a corner, "I've just had the press at my door, Alison, what the fuck?"

"Come straight to my office Jim, don't talk to anyone, don't stop for anyone," Alison was delivering an order. She disconnected the call and Jim continued his journey. He thought about the times that he would bully Malcolm's sister, Isabella. There was never a need for it, she had never done anything to deserve it and yet he lead his little gang to beat on her, torment her, psychologically push her to her limits, and then Darren's acts pushed her to the point of swan diving off a twenty storey tower block. After that, he left his gang, his friends, he knew what he had done was evil, and he realised he had not been punished for it. He had tried to live his life honestly and deliver the right justice as often as possible, and he had been good at it, and as a result, had almost forgotten about her.

He couldn't keep his mind off of that chair. There was a pregnant, innocent woman and her unborn baby that needed him to commit suicide to save them. His brain kept throwing in random thoughts of getting a call that Malcolm had been spotted, or that Lisa had been found alive and well, with no Malcolm in sight. His logical thoughts were trying hard to squash the irrational ones, he knew very well there would be no luck involved. But he also knew he didn't want to die.

The phone rang again, Brad. "Brad talk to me."

"I'm at Ash's apartment, Jim" He sounded almost relieved, "We have her mum alive. There's been a serious struggle here but she is alive."

"Anything we can use?"

Brad drew an audible sigh down the phone. "Jim, we'll speak to the neighbours, and I'll let you know if anyone has seen a vehicle. Once I leave here, I'll head to the Yard." That was a small consolation for Jim to hear.

"What about David Sutherland?" Jim asked, conscious of the fact that in the thirty minutes that he had been awake no one had mentioned him.

"Malcolm posted his whereabouts on the video, probably didn't want to risk being spotted dropping him off if he had Lisa too." Brad stopped as he mentioned Lisa's name. They were close, since she and Ash got together he had treated her like a surrogate daughter, it hurt to think of her in danger.

"Where was he?" quizzed Jim.

"At an outhouse of the Sireon office where he used to work."

"Fuck, fuck," Jim was annoyed, as the week had unfolded he had cursed himself for checking in all the wrong places, or not checking closely enough. "Ok, I'm almost at the Yard, Alison wants me obviously. I'll see you soon Brad."

As he entered the carpark at the Yard, he could feel the stares of the various officers doing their jobs, pausing briefly to stare at him, all of them condemning his teenage actions and asking themselves the same question. Would he do it?

Sunday, April 16th, 10am

The meeting in Alison's office was solemn. The investigation into Malcolm's game this week had failed on all counts. The people that had died, the people that had lived, none of it had been impacted by any of the police involved. They had been dealing with a simple an effective plan, one that had been designed to stir a nation from slumber. Designed by a man who had seen his sister tormented into suicide, abused by a trusted adult at a youth centre, seen his best friend die and two men profit from his death, humiliated in public by a beautiful woman, witnessed a man beat his wife and a son treat his own father like an unwanted pet.

"What's your relationship with Malcolm, Jim?" Alison asked. She looked at him with sympathy. Whatever the fuck had gone wrong with this investigation this week it wasn't time to start pointing fingers. She knew that Jim would sit in that chair at 9pm. She knew that Malcolm would not be found.

"You know a bit about my past, Alison," sitting in the clothes he had slept in, he sipped hot coffee. The shock and pace of the last couple of hours hadn't given him any time to feel a hangover, but he knew he needed the caffeine. "Malcolm and I grew up on the same estate, were at the same school. I didn't recognise him when I first saw his face, it was twenty years ago. His name back then was Malcolm Steele, not Povey, we did some checks. Steele was his mother's name, she died when he was in his early twenties, and Povey was his father's name. He changed it officially through Depol which is why I didn't recognise the name either." He took another sip, looking at Alison as he continued his story. "I used to torment both him and his sister, the woman Nicola, she used to run with us sometimes, she had a particular dislike for Isabella. One night I believe Isabella was raped by Darren Alderman, the man and his family were victims in the basement house. I was working out dates from my memory, the night Isabella was raped, we had attacked Malcolm and he was arrested with some of my gang, but I legged it. I think Malcolm was in the cells when Isabella took her own life."

"Fuck sake, Jim," said Alison, looking at her friend and former lover. She wasn't accusing, but she was shocked. "When did you put all this together?"

"The other day," he continued, "Malcolm used a phrase that jolted this memory, I thought it was weird that I knew Nicola, we hadn't seen each other since back in the day, but when I worked out Malcolm's name it all came together. He was skin and bone back then, not the man he is now." He paused, finishing his mug.

"Alison, he's targeting me because I prevented him from being there for his sister when she needed him the most. And when I was questioned nothing happened, I moved on, he never did."

"What are you going to do?" it was the only question she could ask him. She had asked that question about the other so-called victims this week, she didn't think she would ever be asking Jim to answer it for himself. He had been looking at the floor, trying to focus his own thoughts. He looked up at his friend and shook his head slowly, with almost a shrug of his shoulders.

Sunday, April 16th, 6pm

He had stood alone in the locker rooms at the Yard for more than an hour. Alison had managed to find him a change of clothes and a kit bag. He had spent at least half an hour stood in the shower, stood there with the water pouring over him, trying to control his mind. He thought back to the meeting with Alison, as it ended she had hugged him, held him tighter than she had since they were lovers. He thought back to the coffee he shared with Brad, sitting in his office, Brad has not blamed him, he understood that kids can be assholes, and he had not asked anything of him with regards Lisa. They toasted their coffee cups to Ash and sat for a long time in silence. As he turned off the shower he grabbed a towel and headed out to the sinks, looking straight ahead in the mirror. His face was tired and grizzly. He grabbed the shaving foam from the kit bag and turned the hot tap, wiping the steamed mirror with his left hand. Lathering his face he took time with his shave, catching every hair with slow, deliberate movement, drawing the blade up the length of his neck. Splashing the excess foam from his face, he stood, hands leaning on the sink, staring into his own eyes. He grabbed the towel and dried his face, standing naked in the empty locker room, trying his best to keep it together. The suit was clean and pressed, a nice white shirt and tie. Once dressed he slipped his feet into the black slip-on shoes, taking a comb from the bag and some wax. He set his hair perfectly and straightened his tie. The image of Lisa with silver gaffer tape over her mouth flickered into his consciousness. When he had watched the video, he could see the fear in her eyes.

Leaving the locker room he headed to the car lot. On the way, every officer stopped and looked. Very few spoke. The silence they offered, and the looks on their faces, were either of sympathy or respect. Brad had done a good job of rallying the troops, cancelling out the doubters in the room. Brad wanted them to know that Jim was a decent man. As Jim entered the carpark a car was waiting for him. Leaving Scotland Yard in the back of seat of the car he looked over at Brad, sitting quietly next to him. There were no words exchanged as they drove through London and approached the square. Jim looked over at Brad. "Catch this fucker for me." Brad nodded, and they both climbed out of the car.

Jim was proud, upright and smart. He shook Brad's hand and he turned and began to walk slowly toward the all too familiar chair and the gun resting on its seat. As he reached within a few feet of the chair he heard Brad shout, "Jim!!" He swivelled his head to look at Brad but simultaneously heard the screams coming from his left. The crowd was parting and armed officers were running forward across the square in the same direction, guns raised. Jim couldn't initially see what was causing the commotion and then his eyes focussed, and he saw. Walking towards him was Lisa, her mouth still gagged, her hands handcuffed in front of her. Holding her closely from behind, with a gun in his left hand, pointed at Lisa's belly, was the all too familiar face of Malcolm. He had walked boldly through the crowd, the riot police had parted like a sea for him, and they were now within feet of Jim. Eight armed officers stood in a circle around Malcolm and his prisoner, moving with him as they continued walking towards the chair. The lead armed officer was shouting for Malcolm to stop and drop his weapon.

"Malcolm, no!" Jim shouted. "Don't hurt her, please, don't hurt the baby." He walked towards the two of them, looking at the armed police, "lower your weapons," he commanded, the lead sergeant looking back at him, shaking his head. "Lower your goddam weapons," he shouted this time.

The armed officers one by one pointed their machine guns at the ground. "Now back up," Jim continued to try and take control of the situation, "back up before she gets hurt." He was looking around at the eight officers. "I want you at least fifty yards away." They hesitated. "Now goddammit." The lead sergeant signalled his men with a nod, and they began to back away, still facing Malcolm, still with their barrels pointing at a forty-five-degree angle towards the ground.

Once the armed officers had reached a safe distance they stopped retreating. Malcolm scanned them, not easing his grip or moving his gun. "Jim Ford," he shouted. "The great Jim Ford." Malcolm was smiling, grinning with ecstasy that he was now face to face with the man who had tormented his sister. He looked to his right, Brad had gotten close. "BACK OFF," he shouted to him, "Back off or I'll kill them both." Brad took a couple of steps back. He caught Lisa's eyes, he tried to tell her she was going to be ok.

"Back off, Brad." said Jim, he tried to get Malcolm's attention. "I'm here Malcolm, and I am ready to pay for my sins." He leaned forward and picked up the gun. Malcolm instinctively drew Lisa closer.

"Sit … sit on the chair," Malcolm ordered, holding the gun firmly against Lisa's bump, "I wanna see this, Jimboy." He said the name "Jimboy" with a snarl in his voice. "You beat my sister, you beat me, and you think you can get away with it?"

Jim did as Malcolm wanted. He picked up the gun and sat down. His hand was shaking. He looked over at Brad and the officers.

Brad had his arms slightly raised as if keeping the barrels of the machine guns aimed at the ground about forty feet from Jim. He looked into Lisa's eyes, she was petrified, and they were red raw, tears streaming over the silver tape. Jim flinched as the first of the chimes rang out.

He looked at Malcolm, stared into his eyes. He tried to decipher a weakness, his brain kicking up a million impossible options for him. The second chime rang out, he felt panic.

"JIMBOY!" screamed Malcolm, pushing the barrel of a pistol he was holding into the side of Lisa's belly, making her squeal from beneath the gag. "Are you going to make me kill her?"

Jim's mind focussed quickly. He knew what he had to do. The revolver tightly gripped in his hand. He slowly raised it. The third chime, he didn't flinch, his mind was surreal, and there was only one option now. He placed the barrel against his temple, took a deep breath, and pulled the trigger.

As Jim's body jolted sideways off the chair, Malcolm released his grip on Lisa, lowering his own gun and dropped it to the ground. The man who killed his sister was dead. He felt light-headed, and he dropped to his knees as Jim's body slammed into the slabs, releasing Lisa as he did. Brad and the armed officers instantly advanced, as Lisa stared down at the gun at her feet. She crouched down, one arm around her belly, oblivious to the yells from Brad, grasping the handle in her right hand and returning to her feet. Malcolm was transfixed on Jim, as Lisa placed the trigger against his temple. He knew what was happening, he knew the game was ending and it was his turn to suffer. She screamed, this man had killed her husband, and in the blink of an eye, the bullet ripped through his skull a split second before Brad reached Lisa. Malcolm's body kicked sideways, blood spraying as the bullet left the far side of his head. His body collapsed in front of Lisa, as she lowered the revolver. Brad carefully pulled the gun from her hand as armed officers crowded over the two bodies.

Brad held her, he could feel her trembling, using his free hand to loosen the tape. "It's ok my girl, it's ok." The crowd had fallen quiet, officers moving in all directions, as Brad cradled Lisa. Her baby was safe, but the week had meant they had both lost so much. Her baby without a father, her without a husband, and he had lost two of his best friends. Malcolm's body lay on the same paving slabs as his friend Jim, their blood staining the ground. The game was over, and whether it was right or wrong, Malcolm had avenged the death of his sister and brought the people from his past into the very present. He helped Lisa to her feet, she was crying, and a couple of paramedics in their green uniforms were sprinting in their direction. They took Lisa from him, throwing a blanket over her shoulders. He watched the sweet girl as she was escorted away, wandering if the fucked up justice system that had led to the death of her husband and resulted in her killing a man, would see her charged and convicted.

He looked back at the two bodies as they were covered in blankets, and then over at the media. There were dozens of camera crews and reporters who had just broadcast the death of a good man to the world.

Printed in Great Britain
by Amazon